Seasons of Ordinary Time

Seasons
of Ordinary Time

Stories
by
Robyn-Marie Butt

The Mercury Press

ACKNOWLEDGEMENTS

The author wishes to thank Colin, the Canada Council, and her family, for
financial support that permitted time to complete this book. Thanks also to Nino Ricci.
Special thanks to David Gustav Fraser.

Stories from *Seasons of Ordinary Time* have previously appeared in: *Impulse* (New City Fiction Issue, 1988); *The Governor's Road* (anthology, Red Kite Press), and *paragraph*.

§

The publisher gratefully acknowledges the financial assistance
of the Canada Council and the Ontario Arts Council.

Cover design: Robert Malyon
Production co-ordination and composition: TASK

Typeset in Goudy Old Style and Frugal Sans by TASK.
Printed and bound in Canada.

Canadian Cataloguing in Publication:

Butt, Robyn-Marie, 1959–
Seasons of ordinary time
ISBN 0-920544-79-7
I. Title
PS8576.A5364E3 1991   C813'.54   C91-094571-3
PR9199.3.M35E5 1991

Canadian Sales Representation: The Literary Press Group.

The Mercury Press is distributed in Canada
by University of Toronto Press,
and in the United States
by Inland Book Company (selected titles)
and Bookslinger.

The Mercury Press
(an imprint of Aya Press)
Box 446
Stratford, Ontario
Canada
N5A 6T3

Contents

For Douglas,
who labours alone.

Sorcerers Apprenticed

Sunlight. Leaf and shadow.

The swallows tilted their sunset-coloured breasts around the white-washed corner of the barn and we slapped our feet over and over in the dust to swoon from being alive when:

each puff roiled softer than silk across our ankles and disappeared on the air.

Missy Hurlbut and I sank honey-pails of weeds into the heat of the rotting manure-pile. There the internal combustion of so much summer turned to dung cooked them magically into stews to feed men we imagined we had: tanned dirty men, muscled from the fields, who clumped home to our imaginary house smelling of fieldstone, of sweat, of the bank of greenery they toiled beside for centuries until the shimmering scent of our cooking brought them home again. They shuffled at the stone wall where the swallows now hung twittering from a wire and we fed them from a mess of ragweed and pigweed, plantain-seeds stripped green from the stem, and corn stolen from the fields squashed off the cob and rolled into cakes to be dried like biscuits on a rock in the sun. Our silent men wolfed our creations and were glutted, we sang songs learned in school and murmured to each other like a married couple over our plank table; a sleek brown mouse came and stole the corn-cakes one by one to nibble in the mouth of its burrow. Ted Fenton came and wanted to crush the mouse with a stone but somehow, in the sun and haze our feet planted firmly in the moist warmth of the manure, we prevailed. The three of us hovered above the mouse, breathless, watching, mournful of its frailty because Ted hadn't crushed it. The sun made love over our bare backs. We were apprentices and it was our sorcerer.

For apprentices the day never ends except in a grief of red sky and crickets beating the grass. Then stars prick out— prick out— prick out— pins in the celestial map of our bodies, each white dot a joint in our gangling limbs, a join from our sky to lost suns, from day to the pear-trees wrapped dark-green by dusk. Honeysuckle crouched along the bank of the pond. Its scent towering into the night was a serpent we navigated the darkness by: to strip off our clothes, expose our white buttocks, bare clefts between our legs, dive into the sky and stars shivering at the end of the dock. We held our breaths; the night in its bowl raced towards us like a suffocating and breathless presence; our heads scattered constellations and white dollops of splash caught in starlight like flashbulbs exploding, we were plunged under, we broke surface again: night trapped us inside its dark glass like fireflies.

Later we lay on our backs, our elbows in the mud by the bank, our hair drifting back into wild mint and arrowhead and jewelweed. The warmth of the shallows where sun had feasted all day lulled us, the small heave of the pond to and fro at its edges rocked us drowsily. We talked to each other, not to fall into the immensity of sky. Still as we were we already hung in its image, stars lapping over our shins. Missy's father had shot himself. There was still a hole in their screen door. Later someone had hung one of their piglets with a rope from the striped swing-set and Missy saw it: albino lashes lowered half-way over its bloodshot eyes, its small tongue clamped between its teeth, its nose trailing a dried dark trickle of blood. It had peed on the seat of her swing. She wouldn't swing there any more until her brothers moved the swing-set to the back yard: it smelled of piss and death and they'd taken down the rope but it had burned some of the red paint off the cross-bar when the pig swung back and forth. Missy wondered if it screamed, and why she didn't hear it.

"Maybe you were asleep," I said, "or maybe you were awake

but you were thinking of your Dad."

No, she said. But she might of been asleep. That might of been the time she was dreaming, about standing in the driveway of a big dark house.

"Didja go in?"

Ugh, why would she?

"But in dreams sometimesya haveta do stuff ya don't want."

But she'd wakened up instead. It was morning and just then her brother came running upstairs yelling to her the piglet was hanged outside her window.

"Ugh, was it?"

Outside but down below, it wasn't like they did it right beside her bed.

"Ugh, but still."

We rocked in the liquid sky. The damp breath of mist floating towards the end of the dock smelled of still water and algae and fallen honeysuckle blossom.

"Why'd'e do it?"

Who? They never knew who it was.

"No, yer Dad. Why did'e?"

The sky, punctured, met the pond. The trees flattened inward. We were two hemispheres, the hub of a wheel: whirling, frogs and heron croaking at the knuckles of our spokes.

I don't know, she said. It was raining and he couldn't find anything good on TV.

"Y'mean you were there?"

No, that was earlier. Then her and Allan went to Taits' to chase their baby ponies and Ricky and Wayne went into town to the Southside for a beer because it was Saturday. And her Mum went ta Bingo.

"By'erself?"

Yah he never liked it. He don't– he didn't smoke. And all those Bingo ladies and people they smoke.

"Where?"

Hickson United, in the basement, she thought. Where they have the Strawberry Supper in June.

"Oh." I spooned water over my nipples with my fingers. "An' then'e did it, eh?"

I guess.

"You meanya chased Taits' ponies in the rain?"

Sure, when it rains they can't see you as easy. You can sneak up. Allan jumped on one, but it scraped him off under a thorn tree.

Missy sighed. I thought in the smoky church seven miles away of Mrs. Hurlbut, crouched over piles of red strawberries. They burst against her skin under the cigarette-smoke and the cries of the Bingo-caller. In town Ricky and Wayne drained huge goblets of beer, silver in the glasses and they crushed the emptied cans with one hand each. Three farms down Missy and Allan ran in the downpour after the swishing white tails of the ponies, the babies' grey brushes flicking mud onto their outstretched hands. They ran and ran, over the soaked and trampled grass. At Missy's house, in the porch where the rain hammered like machine-guns on the tin roof and wept down the screen walls Mr. Hurlbut cursed the flickering tv. and put his gun against his stomach where the pain was and pulled the trigger.

He woulda died anyways, said Missy. "Yah. Anyways, we all die sometime." But I wasn't satisfied. I spooned water over my nipples, between my legs, and I needed to know. "Didja bury'im?"

Course.

"Where?"

Back behind the toolshed.

"Is there a cross?"

No.

"There should be a cross. C' we go see?"

What.

"Go look at it. I never saw one before. A place where a body's buried."

It's too dark now, she said. *It would be scary.*

I shivered. "That's all right. It's all right scary. I dareya."

No, said Missy.

"I dareya because it's sposeta be scary an' it's gotta be scary an' it's a dead thing an' it's night an' there might be a ghost, an' we could see it an'– " *No,* screamed Missy. She sat up in the mud screaming. *No, no.* Her thin brown arms winnowed the water white, snuffed out the stars or shivered them big as footballs while her long hair flung down her shining wet back an arced curtain of pond water, a trail of silver strawberries and beer, a dribble of gleaming bullets down a screen.

I burst into tears.

She said, *You* don't know *what it's like fer yer Dad ta die.*

After a while we'd stopped crying. *Okay,* she said. *I'll showya.*

We crossed continents of hayfield and orchard, past the rotting barn looming in the weeds. The gravel road rolled under our bare feet and crickets clicked from the cut-grass by the creek. The ponies in Taits' field were pale shapes hulking silently: the smell of horse came to us on the air like a breath from someone else not yet sensed on waking.

As we went up Missy's lane I got cold. We held hands. The wind chimes by the corner of the house tinkled faintly in the breeze. The dew-soaked lawn met our toes and then the long weeds beside the toolshed. Our hands convulsed against each other. Our eyes ached open wide. The stars leaned over the wheat field that stretched behind Hurlbuts' toolshed and the house. And then we smelled it. We stopped like one animal, peering and sniffing four-eyed, four-nostrilled into the wall of dark against the shed's rear boards. Fresh dirt. Clay loam turned up and piled. Dank, thick, ravishing: clotting in our nostrils, richer than cauldrons of chocolate, heavier, muskier, than the scent of men. Oxford County: a smell like the skin between a horse's back legs.

That's it, said Missy.

"I can't see it," I said, "only smell. Let's go closer."

I don't wanta. "C'mon, I can't *see* it." *It's too dark da see.* "Just till I touch it then." *With yer hand?!* She let go of mine.

"With my *toes.*" I groped for her fingers again. They were limp and cool. "Missy. Come *on.*" Her hand closed on mine like a vice and we went forward together into the shadow by the shed, the smell of clay thickening around us, a clinging damp heavy with woodrot congealing in our lungs. My foot touched coldness. There was a rustle and something clammy rolled against my shin. I screamed.

"It's 'is head!" I screamed. "It's 'is *head*."

Then Missy pushed me from behind.

The clay smell rushed up to me. It filled my suddenly lonely fingers and sank under my cheeks like a softly engulfing mouth. Loam plugged my throat, dirt drummed on my chest, I believed I felt bones or half-dissolving flesh attaching itself to mine. I was dying for sure. I was dead already, our day had been my funeral and I had to cry to think of it now, I began to choke on my own end, began–

Just as suddenly, Missy's fist closed on my elbow and yanked me back into the wheat. Her other hand, still dank from algae in the pond, covered my mouth.

Okay okay, she said, *shut-up. It's only a dumb pig's grave.*

"But 'is head," I said gasping. "It rolled– "

That was just another lumpa dirt. "Oh." *You made so much noise.*

"I did not." *You did too, you were yelling like anything.*

"Well you went an' pushed me. Anyways it was scary."

The wheat rustled over us.

Yah, she said. *Was it ever.* We started giggling.

A light came on from the back stoop and a gold rectangle fanned open past the door as Mrs. Hurlbut, her knuckles bent white on the knob, leaned out into the night.

We held our breaths and looked at her. She wore a flowered print smock-apron, the kind you put your arms through and button up at the back, and the flowers on it were rust and lime, colours found only in church bazaars. The light shining through her hair turned it into a frail bird's-nest; she peered out, her sagging body arched against the dark. She lifted one hand to push a strand of hair behind her ear and a thimble flashed from her middle finger.

"Wilfrid?" she whispered hoarsely. "Wilfrid is that you?"

She strained towards us. Her shadowed eyes turned the night into a phantom. Shouting with crickets, the stars leaning down and the wind chimes tapping by her shoulder, four eyes wary under the nodding heads of the wheat, the night shut itself against her. Refused, she stood for a moment. One soft sob brushed the side of the shed. The gold fan of light closed on itself and the door clicked to on an empty step. Something tugged my foot. Missy was crawling away into the field, swaying the stalks to and fro as she went. I followed. *Wilfrid* was Missy's dad.

When my mother called Mrs. Hurlbut, Missy's brothers were sent to bring us home. We were easy to find. Our shouts of laughter echoed like the cricket telegraph out of Taits' pasture up and down the concession between our farm and Hurlbuts' house.

"Awright you girls," called Ricky. "C'mon home an' quit buggin' them ponies. C'mon."

We screamed and ran away so Wayne would crash after us along the ponies' trails. He caught us and carried us one under each arm, giggling, back to Ricky where he waited by the road. Ricky sucked softly at a beer bottle. When he tipped the bottle up his black silhouette cut itself into the stars.

"Geezes," said Ricky. "Youze two're worse' n boys." He took me from under Wayne's arm. Missy and I rode home on their backs and they pushed us as we clung together on the red swing-set where the pig had hung: back and forth, squealing and shouting, our constellations swallowing us and receding. The pig, now buried behind the shed, had swung back and forth like the pendulum of a clock. Tomorrow in the same arc there would be sun again. We could smell it: in our skins, left over from today.

Eye of the Beholder

The rich boys in their leather jackets drive their Mercedes-Benz. We sit in the back seat alone and there's nothing we can hear above the music. But our eyes are wide. We see the cracks in the upholstery. We see the cross frozen far from us at the end of the black hood. We see the rich boys' souls in the dash-lights of their Mercedes-Benz.

We are drunk. We are drunk and weave down the street when we walk, our voices are thick, our mouths numb around the words forming in them. The rich boys don't show their drink. In the rich boys, liquor glows like blood. Right now we are drunk and wandering in our minds, riding a crack in the red leather under us, riding the rich boys' black Mercedes-Benz. One is at the wheel and the other is beside him. We can't find the humanity in the rich boys, we know them but they have lost their meaning. Their Mercedes-Benz will carry us, all our human components, safe inside. Our souls are in storage in a black freezer.

We're going to drink absinthe. One of the rich boys has an aunt in Spain who owns a bar. The uncle knows where to get absinthe. Somewhere in Spain it's still possible to get absinthe, the kind that has been illegal for a long time. The rich boy sent his friend to Spain with directions and requests. Now we sit in the back of the Mercedes-Benz and see Bohemians sipping from tumblers outside cafés. We imagine Paris sun, artists swathed in scarves, the tilt of dark berets, the tilt of crowds bowling down the promenade. Do the rich boys see this too? We don't know. The crowds are rich with laughter and their laughter is the colour of absinthe.

"Jesus– look out or you'll hit those people." We swerve onto the sidewalk and off. The rich boys drive to an apartment and we go up a flight of stairs, our drunken feet whispering unevenly on the carpet. Mariel is waiting for us. Her large mouth, when it smiles, is like a broken bowl caught in a headlight. We see something stretch out behind her eyes. The rich boys may see this too. They say: "She has that kind of look that says: 'Come fuck me'."

Mariel speaks quietly. She invites us into the dining-room where we sit at an empty table. It's black. Everything in the dining-room is black or grey or white, except two triangles of turquoise glass on the table, and a bowl where a goldfish nudges frantically against the rim. We sit in the chrome chairs and Mariel curls up at the end of the table. We are silent, watching the goldfish dart behind the glass. "He'll be neurotic," one of us says, "from living alone." We watch the fish and for the second until Mariel speaks we think about cruelty and loneliness.

"Oh..." says Mariel. "There was another exactly the same but a friend wanted it." She puts her fingertip against the bowl and moves it back and forth. The fish follows with his nose. "See," says Mariel, "he watches me. I do this every day so he won't be lonely."

"Did they bring the stuff Mariel?" says a rich boy. He is the singer in a band and he and Mariel live together. Mariel also sees the other rich boy, but the singer knows him, he doesn't care what they do: he phones to tell them when he'll be away all night.

"Did they bring it, Mariel?"

"What?"

"The absinthe."

Did they drop it off? Who are "they"? we wonder. The rich boys must know. Pick-up men with black gloves and suits, strangers with Spanish tans. Mariel goes out to the kitchen. "Here it is," she calls softly from the other room and we are picturing the bottle, tall, clear, narrow, amber liquid running in it like an hour-glass. "Well bring it here!" says the singer. He gets

up and dips his hand over the black sideboard. It comes away '
dripping glasses, a stem between each finger. He goes out to the
living room.

We mean to go out but we wait for Mariel. Something whines
above audibility in the kitchen. When she comes out we are the
first except her to see the bottle. It is squat and green.

"What's that whine?" we ask.

"Isn't it terrible?" she says. "It's the refrigerator," and she takes
our hands and we go into the living room, where the rich boys
have taken off their jackets.

In the room they seem fixtures for an elegant monument, dark
statues in the white and grey. Pink neon follows their limbs in
the dove-coloured chairs. The wine glasses stand on the end
table. We look at the rich boys and we believe we are in church,
new Renoirs in the silence before our births, new Toulouse-
Lautrecs in the light on the dark boulevard; and Mariel pours
the green absinthe into our glasses. We wonder: Will the glass
hold it? Absinthe, heavy with our expectations and our boredom.
The rich boys are assured in their boredom and do not wonder.

"Only a mouthful," says the singer. "It' deadly," and he picks
up the glass. He carries it to the mantle and stands beside a dead
branch in a vase and holds his cup up to the neon sculpture and
leans against the wall and downs it. He becomes smooth, like
absinthe: he is a rich boy come into his inheritance, a rich boy
squandering his inheritance with us. We drink while he gets
himself a beer and returns to the wall. Mariel curls on the rug.

"Want to go out?" asks the other rich boy.

"I don't know. Where?"

We think. Someone wants to see a band. Someone wants to
dance. It takes a long time.

"Oh," says Mariel, "I have to stay in– I work in the morning."
When Mariel says no it is the murmur of a pigeon. Her answer
hangs in the room. We think: How can you argue? But the rich
boy says, "You want to go, right? You're kidding."

"No."

"But God, Mariel– "

and then we hear the sound of something pouring in the room. We look at the singer in the corner. His face is glazed and blank and the beer in his hand has revolved neck-down. From it a gold stream bubbles into the rug. Its smell is fresh and sour. We smell this and the rich boy slides slowly down the wall onto the floor and then we notice how things are, how things have evolved: cavernous light, shadows with language, faces wearing their own disintegration. Someone runs out and vomits in the kitchen. We sit still in the room, growing heavier.

"You cunt," says a shadow by the wall suddenly. He's blurring. "*You never fucking change.*" He points shaking at the unused glass on the table.

"Hey," murmurs Mariel. "Hey, don't be stupid, are you all right?" We don't move when he lunges from the wall. We believe he may kneel or pray. The glass sails through the air spinning, pink neon in its stem. It explodes over the fireplace. His shadow falls against the table, his head cracks on it like a stone that rolls away into the room. Something red puts a finger tentatively out from his mouth and then spreads past his chin, a red trail across his cheek gathering on the carpet. We think it is a painting being born. It is paint spilled from Monet's brush, soon it will multiply, the floor melt half-green and a field of poppies stand up out of the room. Mariel uncurls. She runs into the shadows. She kneels beside him and becomes indistinct. We notice how poppies adhere to her fingers.

The other rich boy comes back. He tilts into the room like the broken arm of a windmill. He is shouting. We don't know what he is saying, he has invented speech for the occasion. He stumbles at the bottle and picks it up and the bottle becomes malevolent, insinuating itself into his face, until he crumples and there is silence, everywhere. The chairs are turned up onto the tables. The light is turned out over the flowers and the field. Glasses have rolled or shattered on the cobblestones and the cobblestones, we see now clearly, are human: limbs generating and decaying, heads without eyes, twisted necks and hands, a film of vomit. All of it rots and becomes absinthe, and we draw the thick green oil out of the earth in bottles.

Then we run. We run from unknown artists seated sadly under the Arc de Triomphe, from receding neon and steps pulling out under our feet, onto pavement and into blowing snow. Under a tree stands someone's car. They have left the lights on. We stare at it and our eyes are wide. We see the cracks in the upholstery. We see the cross frozen far from us at the end of the black hood. We retch the word absinthe over and over again into the snow.

Someone has appeared. "I'm so sorry," she says. "This has been so terrible. I want you to take these. Here." We look up from the cold. She stands in an attitude of supplication, holding the green bottle and the keys. Behind her we can make out our souls in the headlights of the Mercedes-Benz.

A Vampire Story

Brightness seduced Dr. Stanto before anything else. Sunlight through the sieve of curtains (no flowers– she had chosen them). A spear where they didn't meet. Fractions of trivia illuminated in its blade: dried, scarred, hardened, stained: a gold slice of the room lifted up and out by sun. It shone between molecules so that for Dr. Stanto things became unearthly. When he woke every morning on the couch, he would stare at the creatures created in this sunbeam. That's what I have to make, he would think, and be too fascinated to do it.

After an hour the sun would shift to lie flat on the floor, which was less interesting, and he'd check to see if he had gotten dressed. Sometimes he would discover that he had. Or had he slept in his clothes? Sometimes he tried to judge the state of his clothes in the small high bathroom mirror by standing on the lip of the tub. The danger of this made his heart pound. He always shook a little, balanced on the edge of the tub, one wrist crooked against the shower-rod, head bent to the square of himself reflected above the sink. Usually it was the area of his crotch, the waist of his pants, one shirt-tail wavering its way down his leg. He would look and look. Was he wrinkled? Did he seem dishevelled? The state of his clothes eluded him. Sometimes even possession of his clothes eluded him; he became convinced that it wasn't a reflection of his clothes but a picture hung above the sink, somebody's sick idea of art. The rumpled lower centre of a human being: *Man.*

Then something would tire, his wrist or his sock feet trying to grip the tub, or his brain trying to decipher the area above the sink. Was that his sink? Is that my hairbrush, I thought my hai was chestnut? Very handsome. Doesn't it curl, doesn't Melva stroke it off my cheek, the piece that comes free? I have a picture somewhere– is that my sink? Yes, the razor. Do I need a shave? Is it time to shave yet?

He climbed down from the tub and began to shave. I'm tired out. What time is it? One thing that never disappointed him was his watch. He always forgot who it came from; once he'd remembered and written it down, but he lost the paper. Now the watch said 6:30. That must be a.m. He had just got up. He was shaving. Yes. He was 68 and his face in the mirror looked 80, there were certain things he couldn't forget and certain other things he wanted to remember and didn't. My brother Raoul was a painter. He was very talented and becoming famous in Budapest. He was young and beautiful. Maybe Raoul had the chestnut hair. Maybe it was because of his talent and his hair that the Nazis took him away. He was 26. Dr. Stanto nicked himself shaving. No. He had chestnut hair too, they both did, standing arm and arm in the– oh yes, in the sunlight, outside the turret of Papa's consultation room beside the lilacs. The same pose every year; outside Stanto Private Hospital. The Nazis took Mama and Papa and Raoul away, they moved into the hospital. Maybe the patients left there were gassed too. He wasn't gassed. He wasn't in Budapest. He, George, was in love. He was in love with Melva, the famous danseuse, and had followed her to Paris two months before the Nazis came.

Dr. Stanto got tired of shaving. He checked his calendar by the toilet and decided he could make it to a literature class by nine, if he didn't forget or get distracted on the way. Now he had to have breakfast. The doctor had told him about that. "Are you eating, George?" I'm eating, you pudding-faced Scandinavian giant, you mental-deficient. I'm a man, I'm in love. I need my strength. He told his doctor, whispering: "Melva's insatiable." His doctor looked weary. Dr. Stanto was terrified he'd said something wrong until it came to him that the doctor was jealous. Of course.

He couldn't recall making love this morning. In fact he didn't remember her at all, no waking with his hand cupping her vulva like a corsage. He couldn't recall the ache in his stomach for that damp warm place one finger rested against. He never tired of it. Her own hand was always tangled in his hair. Melva? He went out of the bathroom. This place is cluttered. She must be aging too. He was filled with surprise.

"Melva?"

Dr. Stanto stood staring at all the gold slices of nothing laid out in the sunbeam on his floor. The beam reached his toe now and part of him was nothing too. There was her blanket rumpled by the couch. There was her face lining his walls. Newspaper photos. Flowers. Oh yes. The brightness. Melva was dead. Melva died two years ago and thirteen days. I have been rushing toward you ever since, contorted with terrible feeling.

"Melva?"

Dr. Stanto cried, standing outside his bathroom. Then he fried an egg and ate it and put on his walking hat for school.

When the microscope began giving him headaches he had left research for teaching. Ten years was enough to get used to halls smelling like snow, the tick of chalk under his fingers, its smudge now and then on his tie. The inevitable thud with which students dropped books onto the tables had come to mean welcome things. Concentrating hard, now that he was no longer there, he could feel the extension of moments along the hand of the clock just before it poked the next minute. He could smell slate. He could trace like a cartographer the face of the student in each class elevated like Cain by acne, he could remember until it filled his head and the space around him the perfume a pale gold-haired girl had always worn, a prissy girl with a madonna's face and two shadows, flags to her studying, plummeting down from her eyes. Her eyes, coal-coloured, the absurd and innocent skin, the gold brows, the hair pulled back tight. This was where memory fell apart and became something else, chestnut, gold, in his arthritic knuckle her hair band a test of suffering and courtly tenderness to slide off, and all that gold coming forward like his morning curtains, billowing with sun, and he, George Stanto, his smooth high-boned face brown from the Mediterranean, his mouth open, fainted under its wave.

He had done this with Melva. Actually she had engineered it, though he rarely recalled that now; she was twelve years older than him, worldly, artistic, the famous danseuse: she had been photographed by Parisian artists, she had danced with bare nipples in fashionable living-rooms in costumes designed by herself. It was Melva who lifted his hand to the back of her head, it was she who gave him the illusion, as she always gave when she danced, that the place they stood was somewhere only he could imagine. Then her gamin's smile grew intolerably soft against his lip and he released it all, George Stanto, Budapest, his abandoned biology studies, his family at that moment poised like black pillars for the last time on the walk beside their lilacs. He had saved a few of Raoul's paintings, wrapped in brown paper. Those and his stories were usually enough to tempt the madonna-like students back to his room. He was an older man. Occasionally he made a careful, didactic observation in class. Nowadays, proud young girls liked that.

Dr. Stanto opened the door of the literature class and nodded to the professor. He felt rather than saw the new articles of flesh that drew him to the far corner. He sat beside her. Do I look stiff, am I taking too long to get into my chair? A bell rang discreetly.

It was a lecture on Blake. Dr. Stanto didn't like Blake. The lecture dimmed to a patter in one ear and he stared at the girl. There was the skin, very clear. It radiated a student's temporary exhaustion. Photographic techniques of the time had imbued Melva's skin with just such a muted glow. The eyes were green. The university's pooled anglo-saxon genes left little chance for green eyes but there they were. Her hair. Was it short? He tried to look closely. Will they think I'm peering at her? Looking closer he could feel what he needed, that freshness which rolled off young women like beeswax, the sweet draft from flesh like breeze caught in their hair. The hair. Auburn. It stuck up over her head as if electrified. She was wearing a leather vest: he could smell that too. His eyes followed her legs. Were those stockings? No, trousers. Tight. Shocking blue pinstripes down the leg. The legs, which Dr. Stanto tried not to think about, ended in small brown boots. Dr. Stanto breathed in his own confusion. Did his breath catch? Did anyone hear? I don't care, he thought, smelling deeply, drawing her presence into his lungs. He could tell that he had found someone. Her dress. Her hair. Because of Melva and Paris and his own occasional ability to make connections without judging, Dr. Stanto knew. His knuckles tightened in his lap.

Melva's first dance– the first one he saw– was in a Bohemian salon in Budapest. There were beautiful women in pants and scarves, cigarettes dangling from their unpainted mouths. Aloof young men lounged by the walls: poets, painters, philosophers. In the centre of them all there was Melva, her round thighs exposed and flashing, her gamin's smile winking in her cheeks, her round arms swaying, her hair a halo round her head. She danced what they all wanted and what they were. He, George, formerly a science student (he'd thought so then), of good family, respectable at eighteen, stared and felt bloom in his chest the overthrow of correct, successful, and implacable innocence. Excitement danced for him in a form dazzling with its thousand other unguessed-at forms and George, in spite of science, was filled with intuition. He would never let go. He had found his life. His life spun and bowed and lifted her bright head and smiled at, yes, him.

By the time break arrived Dr. Stanto's knuckles refused to unlock. He was too embarrassed to get up. Usually he and the professor exchanged intellectual probes, the professor's often, for Dr. Stanto, missing the mark slightly but perceptibly. Today he did not try to talk. He felt tired. He thought he saw himself clearly: slim, distinguished in his age, sensuous still: trapped by his locked knuckles, manacled for slaughter. His skin became yellowish, his head lifted crookedly, he was a fungus groping for the sun. Of course fungi didn't require sun. They had no chlorophyll. Bloodless, he thought, impotent, and to hide from himself his own thin scream of rage, he tried again to unclamp his fingers or to look at the girl. Both were beyond him. *Melva*– he thought, and was ashamed. He sat through the rest of the class staring at his hands. It seemed to him that it finally ended because he woke.

He waited until everyone had left the classroom. The girl went first, snatching up her books. She pushed her way through other students and passed into the hall, a black blade carrying Melva's hair, chopped and on end, aloft into the world. Comforted, Dr. Stanto saluted her silently. When the professor had left too, he managed to find his feet after several tries. The class is over George; you were not yourself.

The walk home he stretched out as long as possible. The smell of crocuses wafted between the houses, a smell which Melva had once said imparted dignity.

Next class– he attended religiously– Dr. Stanto did not let the dam break. The girl left to smoke by herself in the hall and he felt compelled by the cloud from her Gitane to respect her privacy. She and the cloud stood far away, musky and thick. He sucked the thought of her smoke down to his toes: he knew it from every recital Melva had ever given. Poised cigarettes, urgent applause.

After class, when the girl was shrugging into a large man's overcoat, he caught her eye and smiled. She hesitated and smiled back quickly. He threaded through the pleasantries. Eager but not stumbling. Not doddering. They walked downstairs together, out and along the street.

"Please do me the honour of having tea with me."

"I'm sort of in a hurry actually. Maybe next week, okay?"

They were at a light. He touched her sleeve. "Oh, but it will take so little time. My donut shop where I go is just here– " and his heart ran a few steps before them and stopped where he felt her capitulation, somewhere in the middle of the street.

"Well... I guess I can if I hurry."

She allowed him to choose the table and to take her coat. He seated her with a small flourish. At the counter he bought tea, finding it necessary to repeat himself three times when the cashier failed to understand his order. "Are you retarded?" he asked the cashier, hoping the girl would hear. The cashier ignored his comment. Could it have been what he'd said? His wording, his accent? Had he used Hungarian syntax? He decided this was unlikely. He was not incompetent.

"Are you a dancer?" he asked the girl, sitting down with the tray. "Do you take cream? Ah yes, so you said. Allow me." He insisted on prying off the plastic lid. Did the cream waver noticeably as he poured? He was aware only of how thick it smelled; even over the shop's chrome and plastic, the thickness seemed to engulf them.

"No," she said. Questions. Questions were good, they put her in a position of gratitude for his interest. She told him: "I'm an actress. Well- sort of. I'm doing a workshop? For free- while I go to school..."

"Ah." Dr. Stanto felt his eyes leap open, a young strong hand open inside him. It was his hand. "You are an artist then! I thought so. My wife was an artist, a very famous danseuse. Perhaps you have heard of her, she gave concerts in Paris." The girl listened politely. He felt compelled to add- she drove him somehow to humility- "It may be hard to believe for you, you are so young. But I was also a very handsome boy in those days." She smiled; radiantly, he thought. But her eyes slid to the window. Shy. Green eyes. Encouraged, he touched her fingers. They were twisting a stir-stick on the table. "You will not take it incorrectly if I do this?" he said. "I do it with greatest respect for you."

She seemed confused by this speech. "Oh no," she said, perhaps too quickly. Young girls, especially shy ones, had trouble knowing their own minds. Still, a victory was a victory. He couldn't afford doubts. Dr. Stanto lifted her sleeve gently and circled her wrist with his fingers. "Melva had such bones," he said. "Strong, but small. Also such white skin."

"You know," he went on, "I am getting old. I know this. I have had many adventures when I was young, my wife was famous in all the salons of Paris. Many terrible things happened to my family: my brother Raoul was a painter, just becoming famous... " For a moment he could recall nothing. He was aware of nothing but a warmth communicating itself against his hand. The warmth travelled through the veins of his arm, on into the whole of his body. Ah yes, this girl. "Now I am at an age where I remember these things clearly. I have great hunger for someone to tell." He was suddenly appalled. What had he said? But it had worked. Her eyes were rivetted on him now.

"I think we, you know, all have things we need to tell."

"You see, you are très sympathique."

"Oh– actresses have to be."

"Melva died two years ago, killed by her doctors."

"Her doctors?"

"They gave her improper treatment. I know this."

"That's horrible."

"Thank you, my dear," he said. He felt suffused with kindness, made magnificent by loss. "It has been the greatest grief to me. I still suffer for it. I am a biologist, now retired. I used to lecture also at the university."

"Oh, I loved biology in high school." Her face lit briefly and he tried not to be frightened by his own momentum.

"There! We are– what do you call this? kin, kindred spirits." His fingers settled quite naturally around her hand. As if they were courting. Experience: Purity. A shutter opened in his body, thinking of her purity. He imagined it like a white flower between her knees. He raised and kissed her hand. Did she draw back a little? No, no.

"This is the action of an elderly kindred spirit," he told her, projecting the greatest amount of dignity, as Melva had taught him. He had been much younger than her. In order to broadcast his love and ownership he had had to cover up his age. He had had to learn an assurance which extorted other men's faith in its legitimacy.

"I am an artist also now," he announced then to the girl. Her interest– he felt it– flared. "Since my wife died," he added. "I have taken up this second career in order not to go mad."

"Oh yah?"

"Melva carried our expression with her into death. I have now had to find this within myself."

"What do you do?"

"I make, what I call photo-collages. Also I am a sculptor– petits plastiques."

"What?"

"Small sculptures, very winsome. I will describe to you one sculpture which I have just made."

"Sure, I'd like to hear."

She was very polite. Her eyes. There was no longer a possibility, he thought, of them sliding away. I have her. What was he to say? Dr. Stanto waited, hoping an idea might come back.

"My memory," he said to fill the gap, "is not so bad yet. Some few things I forget. But not things far back... " His gaze wandered. He felt ill: hungry, maybe. He should have bought donuts but he had no more money. Shame washed over him. Not even enough for one, for her.

"But what about your sculpture?" the girl prodded, twisting the stir-stick again. Dr. Stanto smiled at her, knowing she would mistake his gratitude for approval.

"This sculpture is a piece of wood I collected from the beach, which suggested such a figure to me: a wooden torso, of a young girl, with a– how would you say, very– beautiful ass– " he cupped his hands to show her, feeling it there like melons– "and breasts, so– full– and vagina, perfectly formed."

The girl listened. She was sensible. So far his description had not shocked her. He grew warmer, her hair glowed as he looked across the table, he felt her hand under his palm.

"And situated before her legs," he went on, "there is a so very

27

small beautiful creature, a unicorn, like a goat and also like a horse. And– very clear, so, red: his tongue, out." He paused. "She wears a flower for a hat but unfortunately she has no arms."

The girl smiled hesitantly. She seemed at a loss. Surprised, perhaps. Or so shy? He may somehow have insulted her. She felt jealous, perhaps, of his love for his art. He lifted his hand from hers and clamped it between his legs, shrugging. "I must have such a creature, inside me," he said. "Would you like to visit my studio?"

"I can't now, I haveta get going."

"It is just so close by."

"Thanks but– I have an audition."

"At the end of our next class, I shall propose it again."

"Sure."

Dr. Stanto led her on his arm to the subway. She accepted this gallantry, he thought, in the spirit of a lady. Some people had believed Melva to be no lady but they were insensible to the privileges of success and a capricious will. Melva swept through her detractors with a grandeur that held her airborne. "Impoverished," she told George. He nodded and felt himself grow taller, floating on Melva's arm, their heads amongst the tree-tops and spires. Melva created with her body any illusion, any world. He, George, had no imagination. He was a biology student.

Dr. Stanto squeezed Melva's arm. In his mind they were already at their rooms. The flat lent to them by the photographer, the ancient bed out of which Melva made gardens stand up. He was weak with gratitude. Instead of sleeping the photographer took opium.

His hand was suddenly empty. This was not Melva? No– Melva kept her hair long.

"I have to be off now– thanks for the tea and that."

He beamed and nodded, hoping he had not offended her. She was pretty if skittish. Not because of him? He felt a sudden panic, reaching for her hand with the gentleness he reserved for Melva he squeezed it.

"You are so charming," he said to the girl, and they parted.

Late in the afternoon, sanding a piece of wood into a little monster, he recalled why he had been with her.

The idea of art had actually come to him before his doctor suggested it. "You might take up a hobby, George, your eyes are still fairly good. You'll waste away brooding." Dr. Stanto took offense at the implied lack of talent in the word "hobby." "Hobby" was recreation for the no-longer-useful. What Melva had taken away with her, besides her presence, besides the effervescence of their past enfolding them like Hungarian sun, was Art.

I must turn creative, he told himself, shocked. Still he had had no idea how to begin. Once he'd tried dancing, stripped to his undershirt in the centre of his cluttered room, waiting for inspiration. Gradually his head sank. His legs shook. His chest caved quietly. His words of apology failed and became tears staining his belly.

Then a long time later he had gone walking on the beach. He always felt uneasy at the lake; his presence there was a burden undertaken by his daughter out of a sense of duty. It was one of the mornings when Dr. Stanto couldn't sleep; it had stormed the night before and the beach was flat and wet, stretching out ahead and behind like grey ash. He walked what seemed to him a long way. Waves tipped over stones to one side, on the other birds woke meekly amongst the junipers. The smell of the wet junipers became haunting to him as he walked. Slowly, placing each foot with a prayer to the sand to hold it, eyes two yards in front. Seeing nothing. The smell began to rise in him like a presence, overcoming that of algae and dead fish. It took on form and moved inside, outside, around him.

"Melva?" he said at last, aloud. "Melva?" He hurried on. Around the curve of shore, over a stretch of wet granite that terrified him, until things became indistinct and a field seemed to him to be fading, in and out, through the mist: young sunlight, wave after wave of flowers, above the shimmering junipers a shape fleeing. Its transparency of skin, its flashing eye, its milky presence blurred: Dr. Stanto went faster and faster. Then the grey shore jolted back with a crash. He had fallen against a broken spruce and lay with his face under it in a patch of dry sand.

Staring him eye to eye from the sand was a piece of driftwood. In his strained view it had the miniature rounded limbs of his love. Then the wood took on the appearance of a small monster, slender and malevolent. He paused, reaching for it. Once again it was a woman. He groped at it and held on. His face dropped into the sand. He was too grateful for this gift to move.

Dr. Stanto remembered then about the smell of junipers. Melva stood up in the bath with a jar of chamomile tea in her hand. She poured it over her skin and her body in the steam, the water, the rose-coloured tiles, breathed with a scent like junipers. He sat on the edge of the bidet distracted with desire. Her laugh burbled under the sweet stream of tea and the sound of it tightened like silk around his throat.

Later they'd gone for air by the ocean and she had made him bury her up to her neck on the beach. He spilled load after load of sand over her. When it seemed she must disappear under the weight she stopped him; the last sand ran between his fingers and she looked up and something went still, all action riffled to nakedness under her eyes: she said to him softly, "Please unbury me."

He knelt, trembling a little. With infinite care he stroked back the sand he had just carried, grain after grain, until one white knee and the chamomile smell of her flesh rose up under his hand. He stared at the knee. He understood that with this act he had created her, and that she had meant him to. Then he plunged his palms into the beach after her, his weight dropped onto the weight of sand, his teeth stung her mouth and shoulders sure that now, now he would crush her back into the earth, until she and it filled his arms with flesh and heat and he lay buried halfway with her, seagulls wheeling overhead and his soul toppled in his chest. Somehow under the sand she had taken off her clothes. The clothes twisted about their wrists and ankles, glittering with bits of shell.

Dr. Stanto stood up beside the spruce, the piece of driftwood held tightly in his hand.

"And here is my studio." Dr. Stanto unlocked his door. He held his breath. The girl was silent. Soon she'd speak, full of admiration. An artist's admiration for the chaos of creation.

He led her inside. Here was every description of Melva ever printed, every theatre bill, every photograph. To make his collages he pasted them into frames and surrounded them with dried flowers, pine cones, smaller bits of driftwood onto which he'd glued eyes. "This is my beloved wife," he told the girl. "She was a very famous danseuse."

"Yah, you told me."

"But I am forgetting myself. Please let me take your coat." He felt full of heat as he helped her out of her coat and found her to be wearing a mini-skirt, scarlet tights, a torn man's sweater. She smelled of musk and dryrot. Somehow all this had eluded him in class. He breathed deeply. He could see the shape of one breast.

"I hopeya don't mind if I eat my orange," she said to him, rummaging in her bag. "It's my lunchtime."

"Oh please," said Dr. Stanto, putting his hand over hers. "If you please I will feed you. I am your host."

"Oh- well, thanks. But don't go to any trouble-

"For a beautiful young woman I will undertake great trouble," he sang out.

The disorder in his kitchen amazed him. Crusted pots and plates were piled here and there and grease spattered the stove and wall. Many unaccountable things lay on the floor, which needed sweeping. A toilet-brush, a box of cat food, a dustpan, the sponge-mop fallen out of its corner, loose grocery bags, a garbage pail half-full, empty egg cartons, cardboard tubes he'd saved, to use for something. Melva must be cleaning. She'd emptied the cupboards. He left the kitchen, not to embarrass or annoy her in the middle of her work.

There was a girl standing by Melva's desk. The girl had auburn hair and scarlet legs. She peered at one of his collages. A friend of his daughter's? No, she never came here. There were no grandchildren. Dr. Stanto felt a fearful excitement. The girl must be a messenger. Eventually she would present him with some symbol of vitality and life and his art would become truly great. She was here now judging his efforts, examining his ability to love. The girl turned and smiled at him politely. Dr. Stanto felt himself go pale: she had handed him his own folly with the smile. He rushed into the kitchen and returned with everything he had been able to find: grapes, cheese, cocktail crackers, Danish biscuits, and– he hadn't expected it, but hoped– a tangerine.

"Would you like something more?" he asked, shuffling clippings and lint off the coffee table. Laid out, it was a feast. But she mustn't think it could end there. "Something hot, perhaps? Cooked vegetables, two or four eggs?"

"Oh no, thank you," she said, sitting. Dr. Stanto watched her knees. Where her thigh tightened a hand could slide perfectly. He felt his arm go light.

"Some cognac, perhaps?"

"This is already tons. Thanks Dr. Stanto."

"Tea? Juice?"

"No it's okay really." She took a grape. He saw her hesitate. Was there something, were they bruised too much, were they wilted slightly? "Let me get you some water for them," he said. "Oh– I am so sorry. I have asked you to eat without a plate."

He came back with a stained margarine tub of water, two scored paper plates hastily rinsed. "Now you may dip the grapes into the water," he said. He sat opposite her and watched her eat carefully, dipping the grapes in water, dropping them between her teeth. It was he she washed and ate. Soon he too would be strong. He stared at her mouth for another glimpse of her tongue. Seeing it made him taut with energy. Energy arced in a bridge between them, fired by her childish body, her indolently active heart. Her full lungs, her unappreciated appetite. She would sleep a great deal. Her red hair would make sharp lace around her head on the pillow. One nipple would sneak above the coverlet, one white foot push out over the bed. Melva had white feet. A shadow seemed to stand up over the sleeping girl. Sit erectly, George, he told himself. If you stoop she'll think you're of low character.

"I must show you my gallery," he said to the girl eagerly. "I will tell you amusing stories about my wife. She was a very famous danseuse, very respected in Budapest and Paris." The girl paused and murmured something which he didn't catch. He drew out his scrapbooks.

While she ate he walked along his walls, talking and talking. He toured his tiny room and the past, explaining shelves of wood, picking his way through debris, unrolling old posters. He delivered Raoul's paintings from their brown wrappers, held them reverently for her inspection. She spoke but he had no idea what she said, he felt heady with her presence, she seemed able to burst the walls of the room, her flesh impinge upon the dust and air, upon the spear of sun draped over her shimmering legs. He saw the blood brilliant through her skin. Everything I am I will unfold for you, and saw it: here was he, a young man, chestnut hair gleaming under Melva's arm, here was Melva, draped on the French photographer's broken couch, making the photographer endlessly notorious; here she stood semi-nude in some satirical dance, here they posed sternly outside the opera, here they drank with a prince she'd performed for. Here they were married, their cottage by the Mediterranean, here was Melva just back from the beach– wearing his shirt, her legs sculpted by the sun, her clothes dishevelled in her hand. Here was a newspaper review, and another, and another. Here are the reviews when she took London, here are the interviews from Bohemian quarters that received her with love and open arms, here, here –

He was sitting next to the girl. He felt vaguely that she was changing. It seemed to him now that the sweetness had gone, her smell was sharp and restless. It may be that this was the smell of her desire. It could be that he had wakened in her a longing for his excitements. He was holding her hand, he felt his lips on her fingers, on the soft hair of her arm. Then the arm disappeared and a pile of clippings fluttered down beneath her boots as she moved around the table. He heard her voice.

"I'm getting out of here," she said. Her voice rose a notch. "You're weird. You're a pervert, that's what you are." She turned. "And your wife is dead, okay? You never remember. *Dead.* You're supposed to be learning how to die *yourself.* I mean after a while Dr. Stanto you just have to forget what happened *fifty years* ago. I mean– never mind. Just never mind. That's what I get for trying to be nice." She had her coat on, she was stuffing the orange into her pocket. "Thanks for the food and that. I wish you'd just act your age." Her red ankles and red hair flashed and she was gone.

Silence settled on Dr. Stanto. The silence lifted and sliced him, stained him and held him out like a specimen under the microscope. He looked about. His studio. What swam into focus through the vacuum she left was old. Bald, liverspotted, sallow; a hermit's stoop, fleshless legs. His chest was hollow. Around him his studio shrank to three boxes with low ceilings and close walls, a bedsitter for seniors in a government highrise stapled everywhere with concoctions of his fear. This is my body, this is my world, these are my shadow gestures fixed down beyond your skin. Here, Melva, are your lover's weaknesses, decorated for you. Seeds, dead flowers, beads, paper butterflies, driftwood sanded and painted a little: unevolved creatures of the heart. Offerings. To him, George, deceived somehow by time, by death, by Melva herself above all, they had become fragile and eternal: his comfort, his speech. He tore her from the walls. This is what I do for you Melva, this and this. He heaved her out into the room. I made you and I am dry. The unicorn with its obscene and probing tongue, the grin of his wooden mistress crumbled under his foot. Love, self-love, bitterness. George, he told himself suddenly, her *hand.* You shouldn't have kissed it so soon.

The sun stopped at Melva's mouth in a yellow clipping. Breathing cleanly, Dr. Stanto clambered to the bathroom. This was not him. This wasn't him, surely Melva was taking a long time to shop? His balance on the tub was brave and steady, he looked into the mirror to know for sure, but it was blank. At last.

He said to her: "So this is you." She didn't answer and suddenly he watched himself appear, entire, his own rumpled middle, his face, his chest bending down. Well, he told her, I know one thing for sure.

I, George, know what it is like to be alive.

Darleen

So'e's goin DARLEEN DARLEEN! eh. An' I'm goin *C'mon man, she threwya over, let's get ouda here.* He says NO FUCKIN WAY. SHE'S MY HEART. SHE'S MY ONE AN' ONLY. MY OLD LADY, EH. MY *OLD LADY MAN!* NO FUCKIN WAY. He's drunk a course. I'm preddy wasted too eh, but I'm okay. An' I'm goin *No she isn't, she doesn't wanna seeya. Ya god it? She thinks yer a bum! Whichya are! So take it like a man, eh? C'mon,* an' I tried da haul'im out again. Geez. Standin right'n 'er mum's rosebushes. I KNOW I'M A BUM, 'e says, BUT SHE LOVES ME. SHE LOVES ME EVEN THOUGH I'M A BUM. SHE SAID SO. I go *Yah well she was blind but now she sees.* An' give another haul, an' that's when'e falls in the big bush. What a loser boy I'm tellnya. Wavin 'is arms an' legs around in a heapa roses, petals shakin down everywhere an' me thinkin, Shit this bush is *totalled. Geezes Terry,* I says *Get ouda the fuckin rosebush, okay?* So I finally got'im up, out onda the driveway, at least. So what happens? So *then,* then that's when she finally puts up the window an' hollers "TERRY YER A BUM AN' A RAISIN! GET LOST AN' STAY LOST ER I'LL CALL MY UNCLE PAUL I'M TELLINYA, I SWEAR!" Her Uncle Paul's an O.P.P., eh, big mean bugger. Always hittin on us Friday nights, out on the Governor's Road. (That's past town, eh. Ya figger ya got the town cops beat an' then the O.P.P.'s getja.) Tryna surprise us maybe smokin dope, drinkin in the car. Which by the way I *don't do,* eh. I mean, I don't. Not till I get *ouda* the car.

Cause, like, I promised my mum, eh.

I mean, ya godda have *some* standards.

So Darleen, she slams the window down again but 'e never hears it anyways, 'e's goin DARLEEN, LISSENDA ME MAN, JUST LISSENDA WHAT I GODDA SAY HERE! DARLEEN! LOOKAT THIS! an'e's fumblin in 'is pants an'e fumbles away an' I'm thinkin if 'e does somethin rude down there I'm gonna never live it down. An' so like I'm goin, Geezes, get me *ouda* here. Why're all my friends such *losers* when it comesda girls? an' tryna pretend'e came here by'imself an' I just ended up here too somehow.

It never works.

Fine'ly'e fishes out whatever it is'e's tryin for in 'is pocket but'e just goes an' drops it on the ground an' so then, oh geezes I'm nearly dyin, 'e gets down on' is hands an' knees an' starts lookin for it. Right there. In the gravel. In the dark. I mean.

HERE IT IS 'e says, stumblin'is way up again luckily, so I don't hafda look like a complete fool an' help'im search around, HEY DARLEEN! I BRUNGYA A RING! I WANT YOU AN' ME DA GO TAGETHER, MAN, YER MY ONE AN' ONLY! *Geezes Terry*, I say, *willya fuckin get realistic?* I'M GONNA MARRY'ER, 'e says, STEVE, THAT WOMAN IN THERE? SHE'S THE ONLY WOMAN FER ME! MARRY ME DARLEEN! YA GODDA MARRY ME! An' I'm goin, *Geezes for God's sake Terr, yer seventeen fer god's sake an' she's sixteen whatja gonna do, elope an' live on pogie?* WHY NOT?!! 'e says. An' then'e starts sorda mumblin an' drops'is ring again an' jiss sorda stares down after it, goin *Soon's I get my twelve, man, soon's I gradjuate. I told'er I'd get my highschool first, an' I WILL.* An' I'm goin *Terry, just come on, okay? I godda doobie an' a couple brews, okay? Let's jiss go now.* Cause I hafda admit, I'm sorda wondering what's happenda my van, eh, leavin it parked half in the ditch up by the swamp so she wouldn't hear us drivin up'er Dad's lane. (Her Dad's lane, eh, it's preddy long. He keeps it gravelled fresh; prob'ly so'e cin hear people drivin up.) Anyways Terry's startin da look kinda sad an' if 'e starts cryin I'm gonna be totally embarrassed in fronta Darleen's window an' all. Cause like, Darleen's pretty cool, eh. I sorda godda crush on'er myself. I mean I hafda admit if I was a girl goin out with Terry *I'd* dump'm too. It's jiss, like, he's a nice guy an' all an'e's a great partier, but 'e's kinda dumb sometimes y'know? Okay so, I never had a girlfriend yet really, only talkda girls at school, on the schoolbus an' that (when I still took it, I mean, I finished my van now eh, I drive *it* in, now), an' a postera Whitney Houston, but I always sorda figgered a good boyfriend hasda be somebody you c'n *talk* to, eh? I mean, I figger– since my mum left my dad way back cause'e never talked to'er. It's not like my mum's a loser er anything, so I figger there must be something in it. (I was a little kid, a course I wouldn't remember.) But my mum's cool eh. She says "Steve, your scrawny, butjoo got soul." Her an' me, we sing all the choruses da Whitney Houston an' have a beer whenever she had a crummy day at work er I missed the bonus question on a math test. I always get a hundred, eh, but sometimes I miss that bonus question an' I really like gettin a hundred-an' -ten out of a hundred. I mean, it doesn't make sense, that's why I kinda like it. (My mum jiss says I should be happy with Perfect, more'n Perfect looks bad.) So now Terry's hangin on my sleeve, 'e's jiss practic'ly slobberin by now an' I'm worried'e's maybe gonna tear my jacket. I'll kill'im if 'e wrecks this jacket man, I will. I saved up an' went da T'ronno da get this jacket. My *mum* kicked in even. I mean, Yonge Street, man.

Terry, I says, *if you even so much as scratch this here leather. If you even so much as fog yer breath on one single stud. I'm gonna creamya.*

YA KNOW YER TROUBLE STEVE ('e's slobberin an' *still* hangin on. But I give up. Unlike me Terry ain't skinny, he's *monstrous*. Ya godda have *some* survival instinct eh.) YER TROUBLE IS YA GOT NO WAY WITH WOMEN. An' then'e falls down again, I mean really da God, an' *then*, then, I'm tryna haul'im up again, 'e starts *singin*. I mean really, man. An' then'e hauls me over too. So we're like, right out there on Darleen's driveway, on'er Dad's fresh fuckin gravel straight from the Beachville quarry most likely, straight from the exact spot where we party every weekend in summer prob'ly, there's prob'ly even a few stones here that were lyin under my tires last week, an' I jiss *know* that Darleen's in there goin Holy Geez what *losers* an' callin'er Uncle Paul, who's comin with 1500 O.P.P.'s by now prob'ly, an' Terry's just singin.

. I had my face headin fer the gravel (caught under'is elbow) but I managed da cram a corner a my jacket in'is mouth, eh, sorda muffled the noise. I can tellya I was jiss *prayin*'e wouldn't leave bite-marks. Till I hear this step on the gravel. An' I know fer sure it's'er Uncle Paul. Er at least it's'er Dad, even though Terry said'e's runnin some dinner tanight fer the Rotary Club an' so neither of er parents're home. An' I hear another step on the gravel, an' then I hear

YOU GUYS SHOULD GEDUP, YA KNOW.

An' then I realize we both fergot about Joy.

FUCKIN JOY, MAN, WHATJA DOIN OUT HERE THIS TIME A NIGHT? LITTLE KIDS'RE SPOSEDA GO DA BEDJA KNOW.

Joy jiss stands there. SHUT UP TERRY, she says, I SEED YOU AN' DARLEEN KISSING AN' SMOOCHING ONCE AN' SADDERDAYS I GET DA STAY UP TILL EIGHT-THERDY P.M.! AN' BESIDES, DON'T SWEAR!

But Joy, I go, *it's godda be midnight by now.*

NO IT ISN'T, she says, IT'S ONE-OH-FOUR A.M.

an' then Terry bellows DARLEEN fromwhere'e's lyin semi-passed-out practically, on the gravel, an' I hear the window goin up again an' Darleen's shouting JOY! YOU GET BACK IN HERE AN' IGNORE THOSE GUYS ER I WON'T TAKEYA DA *BAMBI* TAMORROW.

"I'm goinda the Capitol tamorrow," says Joy still not movin. I got myself free a Terry at least, I'm sittin up, feelin fer damage. My jacket, I mean. *See a show?* I ask'er. I'm lookin in Terry's pockets fer a smoke, 'e seemsda be passed out by now, I don't actually smoke but this is differ'nt. I finally get one, but it's broken.

"It's broken," Joy goes. An' I go *I know*, shit, an' she goes DON'T SWEAR AN' DON'T SMOKE. IT CAUZIZ DAMIJ an' then Terry wakes up an' starts singin again, jiss lyin there, an' I start remembering this algebra equation hoping it'll make everything go away fer a while, an' then I jiss get up eh, an' I take ol' Joy's hand, an' I jiss walk upda Darleen's front door an' open it an' walk in. Jiss walk right in. An' there's Darleen, eh, jiss puttin on'er housecoat over this foxy short nightgown that has a pitcher a Brian Mulroney on the front, gettin ready da come out an' grab Joy, prob'ly, an' I'm not too lucid, eh, I guess cause I never seen a girl in'er nightshirt, my mum wears old p.j.'s she scoffed from my dad I guess, an' so I go *Geezes Darleen ya shouldn't jiss leave yer door unlocked like that, anybody could jiss walk right in like a swamp mugger er something.*

"Steve," she says. "You raisin. Whadjoo go an' give'im a ride out here for?"

So I'm not gonna come up with some genius answer at a time like this. So I just say the first thing I think of, *Like, he is my friend.*

Darleen she's pretty unusual really. She just starts laughin an' tells me da sit down at their kitchen table an' me an' Joy cin have hot chocolate, she made two. An' she took off out the door.

I figger she's gonna go waste Terry er drag'im in the house so'er Dad won't drive over'im when'e gets home an' I should go help'er, but first I godda take a leak. So I give Joy'er hot chocolate an' I ask'er where's the can.

YOU GODDA GO? she asks. *Course I godda go,* I say, *I'm not gonna comb my hair at a time like this.* IT'S ONE-TWENDY-NINE A.M., she says. NUMBER ONE ER NUMBER TWO?

None a yer business, I tell'er, *it ain't polite da ask.*

DON'T SAY AIN'T, IT'S NOT C'RECT GRAMMAR, she tells me. So I go "Yah? Well maybe I'm in Grade Ten now an' I know that, okay? Maybe I jiss feel like sayin it anyway, okay?" An' she jiss goes THE BATHROOM'S OUT THERE.

Boy did I need da piss.

An' then I went back out an' there's Darleen tryna drag Terry inside. Darleen, she's pretty big too, eh, (my mum made sure I knew how girls grow quicker so I wouldn't feel inferior an' that) so she's god'im as far as the front steps, but still, it doesn't seem right somehow, her havinda drag'im in all by'erself. After'e went an' ignored the fact that she dumped'm an' came an' stood in'er driveway with a ring yellin an' massackering a good song.

So we god'im in and trieda put'im in a chair but'e fell out about fifteen times (HE'S A SPAGETTIMAN, says Joy IZ'E DRUNK?) so we fine'ly jiss left'im under the table where'e slid the last time, an' then Darleen says "Joy, go up da bed now, party's over," an' Joy says NOT FER YOU IT AIN'T an' Darleen says "No lip, an' don't say ain't" an' Joy points at me an' she goes HE SAYS AIN'T HE SAYS'E'S GONNA SAY IT WHENEVER'E WANTS. "His name's Steve," says Darleen to'er, "so be polite. Now gimme a kiss an' go da bed." An' so she did. I even thought ol' Joy was gonna kiss me fer a second but she jiss stared at me funny an' went GUNNIGHT STEVE an' then went off.

Darleen, eh. She's good with kids.

Kew Gardens

Mr. Richardson woke suddenly in the night because his heart had gone into fibrillation. He had learned this term only recently by sneaking a look at a form the doctor gave him when he complained that his pulse flapped in his throat. "We'll have to do some tests," the doctor had said. The doctor's secretary folded the form and wrote on the outside in block letters: ECHO. "Take this to the hospital," said the secretary. "It's your work order so don't lose it. Give it to the receptionist and she'll show you where to go." Mr. Richardson looked at the paper. He understood that the folding and the word were a code intended to exclude him. He felt that he had been effectively exiled from his own life, both from within and without. On the bus he opened the paper and read: "CLINICAL INFORMATION. ASSESSMENT DE-SIRED: CHECK ONE." There was an X beside "MITRAL VALVE DISEASE," and on the line underneath, which said SPECIFY, "M.V. FIBRILLATION." He folded the paper back up carefully.

However, his fibrillations had never lasted this long. *Life stops when the heart stops*, sang a new, irreverent tune in Mr. Richardson's head. To stifle his terror, which embarrassed him, he took long breaths and watched the headlights of passing cars wheel across the ceiling above his bed. Heavy water seemed to be settling in his veins. He had a fleeting image of his heart as a sightless gull winging erratically towards a brick wall. Then his throat unclenched and his heartbeat began again, horribly fast. Mr. Richardson was not comforted. He was convinced he was still dying, and that it would be discovered in autopsy he had died from Ankha's pill.

The pill had been small and white. It looked like saccharin. "Take this," Ankha had said. "It'll make a new man of you." Mr. Richardson had noticed that Ankha frequently spoke in clichés. He felt proud of himself for discerning that this was a function of English-as-a-second-language. Catch-phrases to Ankha carried exotic messages. Mr. Richardson envied her until he forgot this conclusion and let the surface banality of her conversation irritate him. At this moment, as he lay dying, Mr. Richardson felt only pity for Ankha. Clearly he had missed the message in the pill; they would discover that his death, although inadvertent, had been her fault. How would she live with this knowledge? He realized that for her sake he must take steps not to die.

He considered phoning his son. His son was a news photographer on 24-hour call and had to be reached through a paging service. This would take too long. His son in any case would only phone the hospital. Mr. Richardson could phone the hospital. If he did they would fetch him in an ambulance and try to pump out his stomach. Mr. Richardson could do that himself. Trembling violently he got out of bed and made his way to the bathroom, remembering even in crisis not to trip over the phone-cord. The cord stretched from the wall-plug to his bed: Ankha was given to calling at 2:00 a.m. In the bathroom he retched until his stomach was empty; then he went to the kitchen and poured himself some orange juice with the idea it would keep him from fainting. He shuffled back to bed. He still shook but catastrophe had been averted. He and Ankha could have a good laugh about it tomorrow. This need to vampirize his situation for jokes Mr. Richardson found more reassuring than the gradual slowing of his pulse.

Back in bed Mr. Richardson began to feel ridiculous. He could not have been dying. Near death one became comatose and had visions. There had been no bright light, no visitations from dead relatives, no issuing from a tunnel into warmth and welcome.

Ankha sold flowers outside the subway station. She was eleven but looked eight. She had unassailable eyes, long eyebrows like wings. The first time Mr. Richardson saw her she was jigging from foot to foot behind a cart of snow-dusted roses. Her expression was blank and unexpectant; Mr. Richardson found himself wondering how many perverts had tried to satisfy themselves on her solidity. He imagined the choking back of shamed whispers: they would all, Mr. Richardson was sure, have been annihilated by the strict death of cowardly acts promised in her face. He didn't buy any flowers that time. He had been too astonished at the gap in his experience which he had just discovered and then leapt instantly with such ease.

The telephone rang. Mr. Richardson noted with surprise that it was 4:00 a.m. *Life accelerates with the heart's acceleration.* He had to hold the phone with both hands.

"Mr. R.?"

"Ankha! You're calling late."

"It's early. Mr. R.? I had a dream."

"So did I."

"How's it going Mr. R.? Everything great?"

Mr. Richardson understood from this that Ankha had had premonitions of his attack. She was asking after his health, out of concern.

"Ankha, what was that pill?"

"Speed, Mr. R. Makes you feel good. Gives you energy."

"It nearly killed me."

"Oh yes?"

Mr. Richardson had no qualms about telling Ankha her pill had nearly killed him. In her vocabulary, "nearly killed me" was used to exaggerate a mediocre experience. It denoted extremity of an unserious and potentially humorous kind. Mr. Richardson realized that he thought of all extremity in this way. The private satisfaction he had gotten out of telling her the truth began to pall. But after all, thought Mr. Richardson, what was extremity?

"I won't give you any more if you don't want, Mr. R.," said Ankha. "You okay then? Seeya tomorrow. Bye-bye."

Mr. Richardson didn't know exactly how Ankha placed these flurried nocturnal calls. He had never asked. He believed- although this was perhaps carrying it a bit far, he admitted- in another's right to privacy. Ankha had never volunteered information about life beyond business, except once: the first time Mr. Richardson bought flowers. He introduced himself. She introduced herself and said he could call her a Paki although she was Egyptian. Then her broken-toothed grin flattened and her eyes turned back to their uncurious study of subway patrons. She might be watching TV, thought Mr. Richardson, backing towards the stairs. He was going to meet his son for lunch.

"Hi Dad. Christ you look awful, what're you doing with yourself? Still go to the galleries?"

"I'm not doing to myself William, it's being done. It's called aging, William. I am getting old."

"Dad, for god's sake please call me Bill. You're not so old. Seventy-five isn't old."

"How many of your friends are seventy-five?"

"What? What's that got to do with anything? Have the salad Dad, it's easy on the waistline and high in minerals."

Mr. Richardson had settled comfortably into retirement by devoting his time to his one interest: looking at pictures. He went to one gallery per day. Fortunately there were enough of them that by the time he completed his rounds the exhibits were changing, and he could begin again without having to see anything twice if he didn't want to. At home he kept boxes of old postcards and scrapbooks of pictures clipped from newspapers and magazines. To Mr. Richardson these pictures were in the nature of catalogued passions: each held for him the arrested spirit of a place he would never go and so found beautiful. There was also the satisfaction of shapes, forms, colours in balance: a charred house, a Cape Breton hill, the tinted avenues of the Kew Gardens.

"I covered a murder last night," Bill was saying. "One of those subway stabbings." He took a mouthful of spinach. "Pretty standard. Pool of blood, chalk outline, investigating cops, you know."

Mr. Richardson built himself an idea of this: the white outline of the body on the subway tiles would be graceful. The blood, not yet darkened, contrasted with the dinginess of the surroundings, intersected at a point of tension with the chalk mark. Bill's camera would not see this. None of his son's photographs had found their way into Mr. Richardson's collection so far.

"You can' t be too careful in subways at night."

Nonsense, thought Mr. Richardson. All murders in Toronto are premeditated and have to do with jealousy or racial gang wars. *Those not of the underworld are safe.* His salad came. Mr. Richardson greeted a pause from his heart and stabbed at a sprig of watercress.

On Sundays Ankha visited Mr. Richardson. The occasion of his near-death had been a Saturday night. At 2:00 p.m. the next day Ankha let herself in at Mr. Richardson's door. Somehow she always managed to get past the controlled entranceway without buzzing. Mr. Richardson had forced himself to rise at 10:00 am. so that he would have time to dress and rest again before Ankha's arrival. To appear as normal as possible, thought Mr. Richardson, catching sight of his very pale face in the tea kettle.

"Hi Mr. R. Mr. R., you okay? Let's look at pictures." She rattled in the kitchen, making him a ritual cup of tea. She herself always drank orange juice from the bottle, standing with the fridge door open.

I would have to be really dead, thought Mr. Richardson, before it would interest her. This idea delighted him. He gulped his tea and then got down his scrapbooks and the patent medicine box filled with postcards. He took them to the sitting room.

Ankha was waiting perched in the yellow chair amongst Mr. Richardson's plants. "Too many plants Dad!" Bill had said. "You need a machete just to find a chair." Ankha sat rod-straight cupping her bony elbows. Daylight filtering through Mr. Richardson's plants hit the angle of one cheek and a dark brow. It highlighted her beauty, which to Mr. Richardson suddenly made her look sinister. Still, that belongs in my collection, Mr. Richardson said to himself. She was wearing a turquoise shirt with torn sleeves which she now tugged over her knees. Mr. Richardson decided that he didn't like the shirt. Its too vibrant colour in the window of plants defied him in a way that caused not restfulness, like a photograph, but agitation. He set down the pictures.

"Come," he said, "on the rug."

Every Sunday they went through the pictures. Sundays, Mr. Richardson took a rest from the galleries, the perfect or sometimes flawed division (he could tell when they were bad, although he had no stylistic preferences) of canvas by ink. Mr. Richardson was not one of those elderly who communed with plants. When it occurred to him, he watered them.

"I like this one, Mr. R." Ankha had opened a scrapbook. She pointed to the burned newspaper house. Mr. Richardson rustled through his postcards.

"The Kew Gardens," he said. "I want you to see my Kew Gardens series. They're very old. They're full of flowers. You'll like them."

"Did you live there?"

"No."

She turned a page, frowning.

"Here," said Mr. Richardson. Ankha looked up from the spidery remains of a crucifix in a field. The chapel around it had been torn away by bombing.

"I've imagined an order for them," said Mr. Richardson. "If you were walking there."

"What?"

"Going somewhere in particular. Well- drawn somewhere," said Mr. Richardson. "Compelled. There's a progression. Some of them seem to be leading to others. They get closer to the end as they go along." He was positive from her unbroken gaze that she hadn't understood any of this. He began to feel confused.

"What's at the end?" she asked unexpectedly.

"A pond." Mr. Richardson was elated as if at the sudden imaginative leap of a disciple. "A lily pond."

"So let's see."

His first card was the Herbaceous Border. Discreet lettering identified it in the corner. "See," said Mr. Richardson, "here's the stone path. It goes along beside this bank of flowers towards the trees and turns a corner." Hand-tinted phlox, floxgloves, primroses, hollyhocks, assorted daisies burst beside the line of flagstones. Each tree in the distance had its carefully painted ring of shadow. The sky seemed bright but cool. Spring? thought Mr. Richardson. "See? It turns a corner. It leads you along. It makes you want to turn the corner too."

"What if you want to go into the trees?"

"Well you might but I doubt it. Think how the flowers must smell." Mr. Richardson felt weak thinking of the smell wafting from the Herbaceous Border. He saw a blue evening, dew about to fall.

"What smell?" said Ankha, playing with a strand of hair.

"The flowers." He went on to the next card.

"Here," he said, "here's the Rose Pergola. Rosebushes on trellises. The path leads you around a corner and along this walk under the arbour. Look at them all! Each arch has a different colour. They nod down at you when you walk underneath."

Ankha placed one dirty fingernail on the end of the walkway. "What're those two people?"

"Those are posts," said Mr. Richardson. "It's a gateway. See, it leads you to the gateway. You want to see what's through it. What it's a gateway to."

"What's this house?" said Ankha, shifting her fingernail to the wall of a building etched dimly above some foxgloves to one side.

"It's not a house," said Mr. Richardson, irritated. "A palace, maybe. Or a cathedral."

"What?"

"A church."

"Oh."

Mr. Richardson passed quickly along the wall under the Rose Pergola. Stripes of shade and sun blinded him as he stepped from one blossom-heavy archway to the next. "And here," he said. "This is what the gates open out to. The Rose Garden."

They looked at this picture in silence. Here plots of tinted roses– pink, yellow, white, red– lay scattered to the sides and corners. The centre was grass. Grass stretched past trees to a sky and haze-obscured horizon that seemed to be tossing in a fierce wind. It occurred to Mr. Richardson that he might have gotten the order wrong. He went on quickly.

"Now this is the Rhododendron Dell," said Mr. Richardson. "Rhododendron's a kind of bush. Its flowers look like torn feathers." The path in the Rhododendron Dell was narrow and wound between flaming bushes. The trees further out were low and soft: willows, probably, thought Mr. Richardson.

"But if you follow *that* path," he went on, "you come here. This is the end. It's called the Aquatic Garden."

"What?"

"Water. The plants grow in water."

Ankha laughed suddenly. Mr. Richardson frowned.

"It's a kind of maze. And the centre here, see, here's the lily pond." Inside the stone lip of the pond the lilies had been coloured blue and red. Mr. Richardson was suddenly sure that there were no blue or red water lilies. Only white and yellow. His throat tightened and his heart wandered for several beats. As long as it doesn't fibrillate, he said to himself, drawing a deep breath. A wave that might have been the night before curved towards him. He held it back and stared at the sharp corner of a pool in the Aquatic Garden. Ankha waited for him to go on. Concentrating on the impending wave, Mr. Richardson couldn't think of anything which might communicate a significance in these clumsily retouched photographs to a minority child who sold roses outside the subway. Her silence began to press him. His heart broke into a flutter, it was a tinted gull or red water lily bobbing on the crest of the wave. He wondered why he had never inquired about things that might be important to her.

"When I was three in Egypt the sky was high up," Ankha offered. Then she was no longer looking at him. She rose with a singleness of purpose that seemed to Mr. Richardson suddenly breathtaking and seized the doctor's form which was lying on the end table. A thin line appeared in her forehead as she traced ECHO with her broken nail. Still holding the form she went back to the yellow chair.

Mr. Richardson, watching her, forced himself to draw shallow breaths. Don't make it rush more, he told himself. A beam of light refracted in Ankha's eye as if in a lens. The sluggish water lurched in Mr. Richardson's arms and legs. *I was afraid,* her eye's radiance made him say. *But we of the underworld ought to be safe.*

Ankha froze laced with leaves in his window. His heart on the peak of the wave crumpled into her hands.

Jonas Hunter Died as a Burst of Electricity

Because he was a monk, Jonas Hunter got no sex. Unused, his body became unreal. And so at death this most famous of modern Canadian monks disappeared neither into the ground nor into the incinerator, but straight into molecular energy. Since the discovery of quantum physics, this has been the highest wish of everyone without a body.

At the time of Jonas Hunter's death he was a guest at a foreign monastery. The enraptured monks called him "father" in heavy accents, while he spoke to them about God and the soul. An aura of holiness surrounded him. He pushed himself to exhaustion. Finally between two luncheon and dinner sermons he walked through the courtyard garden– past the vegetables and lilies– to take a nap. It was a hot day. Father Hunter switched on his fan and climbed into the shower. Water leaked past the shower curtain and ran across the floor towards the fan. It spread over the floor in a pool. Father Hunter turned off the water. He padded across the room to find a towel. At the edge of the pool

at the edge of the conspiracy between energy

and matter

his foot found the fan-chord and Jonas Hunter and the fan went down into the water together, both still spinning.

Later the bemused monks found him, their own Last Supper laid out serene and lifeless. They noted the archaic smile his nakedness wore. They pulled their homespun and silence over his face.

His ideal method of death, embodied for them all, was to become one with a burst of energy, lying in the Mother's pool. The water broke from the womb of Jonas Hunter's life and he was born into death as a spark speeding to its generator again.

Because he died before dinner, here is the sermon Jonas Hunter never gave:

THIS STORY UNFORTUNATELY IS CONSCIOUS. A STORY CONSCIOUS OF ITS EXISTENCE WHEN IT IS STILL HALF-CREATED RISKS NEVER BEING FINISHED. IF IT DOES GET FINISHED IT WILL PROBABLY NOT BE ART. NOTE THAT GOD WAS SMART ENOUGH NOT TO CREATE ADAM'S MOUTH FIRST. IN THIS WAY IT COULDN'T OFFER ADVICE WHILE GOD MADE THE REST OF HIM.

EVE, WE WILL LEAVE OUT OF THIS.

What Jonas Hunter would have said was, "Take a miracle. Take Our Lord and a lunatic. Take– " but right here, bright particles would have begun reeling behind his eyes.

behind distracted Jonas Hunter's glasses and his eyes
between the hemispheres of his contemplative mind
between the retina and the cornea
between the receiver and the cornucopia
a shower of incandescing particles.

Recognizing the omen but unafraid, Jonas Hunter would have returned to his talk.

"Take this miracle," he would say, "of a calmed madman. Pigs, excited by the madman's antics, raced madly in turn into a ditch. Peasants watched. And among them they gave a name to what they saw. They saw insanity confronted. They saw Nature routed.

They saw two apparent impossibilities coincide. The peasants opened their mouths and announced a miracle. Their act of faith was speech. In any sequence, the gesture of creation is not the first gesture, but the last."

Jonas Hunter lifted his head and looked over the sea of journalists' and monks' faces. He adjusted his glasses. He sighed.

"Everything is defined," he said, "by its end. Only someone who'd forgotten he's a fool would emphasize Opinion before all the facts are in."

THIS STORY IS MOVING ALONG NICELY NOW. IT HAS MADE SEVERAL POINTS. SO FAR THE STORY'S CONSCIOUSNESS HAS NOT BECOME TOO HEAVY A BURDEN, EVEN IF ITS INTENDED AUDIENCE RE-MAINS OBSCURE.

IT IS STILL TOO EARLY TO TELL, HOWEVER, WHETHER JONAS HUNTER'S GHOST IN HEAVEN WILL APPROVE THIS STORY OR WILL REMAIN CAUGHT UP IN DEBATE OVER HIS BEATIFICATION.

The monks rustled and settled again.

"Sometimes you cry," Father Hunter continued.

"Sometimes the gap between the required and the achieved seems too great to be bridged."

He paused.

"In fact," he said, "it is."

A soft murmur of astonishment went up from his packed listeners. Local dignitaries invited for the occasion frowned imperceptibly as Father Hunter changed colour before their eyes in a subtle descent towards outlawhood. Church Fathers won-dered if he would have to be discussed before a council; they cast about in their minds for the particular bastion of theology he had offended. At the podium Jonas Hunter paled slightly. He took a sip of water.

"But you must imagine," he went on, "how the tears of perpetual failure gather into a pool. This pool– where our face reflects as a rejected portrait– becomes divine source out of which the bridge springs. It may seem," he said, "that God piles our weaknesses like stepping-stones over an abyss He cannot span alone. This is true.

"However,"
said Father Hunter, now swaying exhausted at his podium,
"God is the conspirator who always attends a little death:
"and God's intentions are not ours."

He stepped down to thunderous applause. Foreheads of dignitaries and Church Fathers unwrinkled. There was a unanimous unspoken decision that nothing could be done.

Father Hunter, walking afterwards through dusk gathering in the garden, silently acknowledged a haunting truth. He believed what he said, not because it was often proven to him, but because he had to in order to go on at all.

THIS STORY HAS BECOME SOMEWHAT DICIER, AP-
PEARING TO DISGUISE ITS PHILOSOPHY WITH ITS
IDEA OF HUMOUR. THUS IT SEEMS CLEAR THAT THE
STORY IS NOT ONLY CONSCIOUS BUT ALSO CIRCU-
LAR AND POSSIBLY A HOAX. IT MAY IN FACT INTEND
TO CELEBRATE THAT NARROW AUDIENCE COM-
POSED OF THE TERMINALLY DOUBTFUL.

Father Hunter stopped on the stone doorstep of his cottage, suddenly overwhelmed by the scent of lilies. Bright particles burst once again in a shower through his imagination and he saw them for a refracted second as electrons flowing in the throat of a

flower. They seemed to illuminate the dusk.
   The next moment he said to himself:
   How thick the air is. I must bathe before I go to sleep.

BY THIS TIME– WHICH IS, HIGHLY ABRUPTLY, THE
END THE STORY CALCULATES THAT ONE WILL HAVE
FORGOTTEN ITS ENTIRE PREMISE IS BASED ON MERE
SPECULATION. IT CALCULATES ONE WILL HAVE FOR-
GOTTEN THAT THE SPEECH RECORDED IS A SPEECH
JONAS HUNTER NEVER GAVE. IT CERTAINLY CALCU-
LATES ONE WILL HAVE FORGOTTEN THAT MANY
LILIES SHUT UP FOR THE NIGHT.

   Between the retina and
   between the receiver and
   between the   and

a shower.

A Magician's Manual

Bea's first love was Liam. She was three and Liam was just born; Liam lay in the study in an antique pine cradle as high as Bea's chin. The cradle had four turned posts at its corners to rock him by, and when Bea stood on tiptoe to gaze in, Liam lay there, quiet and mysterious, in a swath of blue blanket. Sometimes he was awake and would gaze back at her. Sometimes he was asleep. Bea examined his large blue eyes, his gold transparent hair, his skin that looked and smelled like milk. Where there had been nothing, there was Liam. Bea couldn't stop running to peer in at him.

Bea's next love was Duncan. Bea was four and Duncan was seven; Duncan set up a box on the kitchen floor after school and on it he reverently placed a bowl of water. He dug a penny out of his cowboy bank, and as Bea watched sceptically he taped the penny inside the bottom of a glass. With a flourish he seated her across the box from him. He paused. Solemnly he invited Bea to push the glass under water upside down until it hit the bottom of his bowl. Bea did: water closed over the glass and crept up her wrist and then wet her sleeve to the elbow. "Now bring it out," Duncan intoned. Bea lifted the glass up again, water pouring off her arm. "And– " he cried– "look inside! Is the penny wet?"

When she peered into the glass, Bea discovered to her shock that the penny was dry. Duncan grinned casually. He took the glass from her and did the trick again, and they sat on either side of the box handing the glass and the penny back and forth.

Then Duncan explained to her the mechanism by which his penny had not gotten wet. Duncan didn't realize that magicians never reveal their secrets. Bea didn't know that audiences by definition are always in the dark. They believed that the explanation was more magical than the trick itself. People who believe this are dangerously hopeful. They are destined for trouble in romance.

Because of this love, Bea chose her first profession. When they grew up she would be Duncan's assistant; they would have a great career, travelling the world and astonishing people.

Bea's next love was one of the workmen who came to lay cement for the stable. By then the Chalmers had moved to the farm and Bea liked to perch on the steps of the patio waiting for starlings; she'd watch which holes in the apple tree they went into, then steal their eggs to sell to her father. He paid five cents. The starlings bullied other birds, and Dr. Chalmers hated bullies.

From her vantage point on the patio steps, Bea could also see the two workmen going in and out of the barn. They were laying a floor. One was blonde. He had a tanned face, bare tanned arms; all day he pushed wheelbarrows of sand back and forth from a gleaming red truck to the stable. It ruined something in Bea to look at him. Discontent entered her world. She forgot about starlings. Bea, age six, became gripped with the idea that she must come to the blonde young man's attention.

For a full day, she agonized on a plan. Not once did it occur to her that the young man might notice her if she did nothing. Finally, she borrowed a white plastic lamb from Liam's toy farm, cleaned a bottle with a narrow neck, smeared the lamb with honey from the jam cupboard, and stuck it in the mouth of the bottle. She marched boldly, trembling inside, across the lawn with this concoction. In a style she would later consider bratty and later still, transparent and forgiveable, Bea, age six, informed the young man that her lamb was stuck inside the neck of the bottle and that she needed him to take it out.

When he had accepted the bottle, Bea ran and hid behind an

apple tree. From this distance she giggled victoriously as her current love, smiling at her in a puzzled way, extracted the plastic lamb. Then, while she watched him, framed by the forks of the tree, he licked the honey off his fingers. The new, ruined thing in Bea pulled her down. It was summer. In the sun his gold hair shone like wheat. He placed her lamb and the bottle diffidently in the grass, while his friend laughed at him. Then he turned away, shrugging, shouldered a sack of cement, and disappeared into the stable. Bea's father raised the price of starling eggs to a dime.

Once discontent had entered Bea's world, it stayed.

Bea's next three loves were television heroes. She was vaguely aware that their scratchy country-TV reception masked reruns, but that meant nothing to her. For the rest of her life, thanks to John-Boy Walton, she loved the sight of a man's arm-muscle in a rolled-up sleeve. For the rest of her life, thanks to Adam Cartwright, she loved the whisker on a man's face. And for the rest of her life, thanks to Captain James T. Kirk, she loved the firm wall of a man's chest.

For the rest of her life Bea regarded television as unsatisfying and fickle, all her TV loves having disappeared when she was 14, without her consent, at the whim of distant executives and the behest of the Nielsen ratings.

Bea's next love was a musician friend of Duncan's. Bea, fifteen, was still welcome any place Duncan went, and she hung out with his friends, where he showed her around proudly, boasting that she never wore make-up. His friends were too young to be hippies but they wore beads, grew their hair, dressed in clothes made of India cotton. It was Bea's first taste of marginal living. "Look at that skin!" Duncan cried. "Wouldn't you want to kiss that skin?" Bea, mortified, nevertheless had faith in Duncan's showmanship. At her first adult party, thrown by

Duncan's friend the musician, Bea sat drinking herbal tea, nervous but marvelling that this innocuous evening would end with her finally learning to neck. Duncan had suggested this might happen, as if to warn her.

Duncan's friends were in a Doors period. Some of them had drawn impressionistic pictures of Jim Morrison as Jesus; they strummed "Light My Fire" and it was full, at least to them, of enduring insight, profound insinuations. Bea's love, tired of his guitar, sat down at the piano and started singing.

Bea's heart, now quite used to its ruination and impatient to be ruined more, turned and stretched inside her. Timidly she perched beside him, watching his white fingers nudge among the keys. She tried, successfully, to imagine them on her body. His cloud of dark hair brushed hers; he smiled at her. Then a girl his own age sat down on the other side of him, and put her hand on his leg.

When they had all gone home Bea lay in bed full of impatience and despair and kissed her arm, for practise.

Duncan still had not learned that a magician never reveals his secrets. Bea still had not learned that an audience, by definition, stays forever in the dark.

Bea's next love was also her only practical one. She transferred her affections to Jim Morrison. Her passion was tinged with caution because he was so much older; but a week later she discovered he had already died, fat and in the bath, heart broken down by drink, and she abandoned him again because that much dissolution was too abstract for her experience.

Bea's next love was the sky outside her bedroom window. For three years, Bea, age 16, age 17, age 18, announced to it nightly her expectation of a man. Boys at school came to her attention and faltered into insignificance when they failed, as they inevitably did, to meet Bea's stern standards for romance. Bea required a man to be intelligent but still entertaining: a combination rare among high school boys.

Bea's next love was her cousin Frederick. With Freddy, Bea, age 18, learned the runnels of her body; became terrified of them; exercised her heart's abysses.

He was not like the others. He was another time, another story.

Bea's next love was a painter in university. His name was Werner. She'd been surprised at first that of all Duncan's friends she was the only one still committed to the arts; but eventually, thanks to Werner, coffee-houses and herbal tea became memories full of insurmountable boredom. Together she and Werner gulped bennies, wore black, ate only junk food, cut their hair and clothes with nail-scissors. They smoked roll-your-owns and shared a tacit understanding that sex was passé in a world run by Ronald Reagan. Werner learned voodoo from a library book. Bea stole spices for him from the campus convenience store after looking up which ones were useful for incantations; once Werner did a spell so she would pass her Modern French Drama exam after not studying for it. When she got her exam back and it turned out the spell had worked, they dyed their hair blue to celebrate. They sat in a litter of paint tubes and full ash-trays in Werner's room, circling articles about nuclear armament, chemical warfare, and cancer. Once a week they went dancing with their friends at a club downtown. They would come back to campus on the all night bus covered with bruises, drenched in their own and other peoples' sweat, giddy from sleeplessness, noise, and booze. These were Bea's glory days. She and Werner lay in his university residence bed, staring, drunk, at the phantasmagoria of junk he had collected for his paintings: broken dolls, mangled toy trains, rusty gears, took on grace in the wash of all-night fluorescent light from the parking lot. Werner had found a can of synthetic whipped cream. If it had been real they would have thrown it back out, but because it was synthetic they took turns spraying it onto each other's bodies. Then gently, tenderly, with courtly modesty, they licked it off again. On Werner's stereo Sham 69 sang in indecipherable London dialect. While guitars crashed they scratched the dots on the scratch'n'sniff card from a Smell-O-Rama movie, trying to name different stinks in the dark. Their laughter erupted and overcame the night, filling the jumbled room with giggles; the silvered ashtrays and heaps of clothes resonated with their delight, their hearts had never felt so sure, they were light, the smell of synthetic pizza dots and pressurized oil-product swam in their heads. This was the second scene Bea would recall before death, whenever Death came: Werner's pale emaciated face, his torn hair, bent over her breast, and his warm gentle unexpected mouth around her nipple. One of them had sprayed whipped cream there. "Is it gone yet?" Bea whispered, innocent. "Long ago," said Werner, also innocent.

They went still, noting the total absence of pain between two who had begun to suspect that in spite of voodoo, theft, drugs, in spite of the hoarse graciousness of an obscure and now-defunct British punk band called Sham 69, pain was what they would carry, like a gold tooth, to their graves.

*The first thing Bea would recall before death was Duncan, handing her the glass with the penny, regal over his bowl of water.

Bea's next love was Guy. He was much older but didn't look it. He first noticed her after a concert in a club where the only way for her to reach her friends across the hall was to walk stepping on the seats of all the tightly-packed, now-empty chairs. To Bea this was practical necessity; to Guy, who was waiting with the others, it made her the inescapable hand of fate scuffing across bar tables to find him. Having noticed her, he fell in love with her next time they met because he couldn't stand the pretension of her shocking-pink elbow-length gloves which she kept on at all times. Things were cemented between them when she turned down his offers of cocaine.

Bea knew none of this at the time, only learning Guy's perspective of events much later. For herself, she was naturally suspicious of him. Guy's drugs were expensive. Also, amongst her anti-sex crowd, Guy was clearly sex in full flight. Guy's blonde hair and skin and his high dangerous cheekbones gleamed with sex; sex poured from the spring of his gait and his lean hips. Looking at Guy's cheekbones Bea sensed that to find herself under them would mean the end of her world, the one where they wore black, picnicked under the wrecker's ball, slam-danced for armageddon lost in poverty and cheap drugs, awaiting doom by their twenty-third birthdays. Months later, her suspicions fulfilled, Bea, age 22 and once more vulnerable, lay in Guy's huge bed and revealed that she'd worn the shocking-pink gloves to hide her mangled knuckles. Two days before he'd first seen her in them, convinced that nothing would ever happen to her, she had punched out a mirror. When Guy heard this, he moaned. He rolled over and slid her into his arms, murmuring "Baby... baby... ." Instantly and forever, Bea relinquished her contempt for this endearment. In doing so she relinquished the part of her Werner had loved: it was the part which would have had to acknowledge that as a man Guy was definitely passé, his endearments those of dinosaurs. Instead Life recorded its first and thus far, only, victory over Bea's intransigence; and Guy's golden voice saying "Baby, baby..." while his great bed creaked like a ship under full sail was the next thing Bea would carry with her wherever she went when life ended.

They moved in together. When he was stoned or drunk Guy spoke softly and ravishingly of marrying her. Bea, still young enough to be sceptical of the future, came to see these dreams as decorative but useless pillows he occasionally tossed around. Then she got sick from oppressive methods of birth-control, and Guy, confused by the spectacle of her physical pain, finally made the choice he'd been leaning towards: he threw over her dismal favours for needles, whiskey, and cocaine. After this, aware they must be destroying each other though they couldn't feel it, they parted to pursue their lingering dreams: his of eloquence chemically induced, hers of love without suffering.

Once or twice Bea had come close to reaching for a knife, baring her chest, but in the end she hadn't. At the bottom of her misery she had glimpsed a shape, also suffering, which looked too much like Guy's; and realized that no-one this unhappy should have to contend with any life but his own.

Bea's next love was Cosgrove. Cosgrove was the first man to meet Bea's stern intellectual standards long after she had discarded them. He also had a cheek dark with whisker, arm-muscles swelling just below the line of a short sleeve, a chest like the prow of a frigate. Nevertheless, Bea had not originally considered Cosgrove for his beauty. Cosgrove wore layers of huge baggy clothes. She couldn't have known how beautiful he was until she had already chosen him anyway. Bea, age 26, fell under the spell of Cosgrove's ruminative height, his Québécois accent when he spoke French, his wit, which made her laugh, his improbable theories about his own dreams and Outer Space. They made love eleven, fourteen times, over one night and a day, in a swamp of sweat, under summer light in a poor part of the city. Seen from Cosgrove's cracked window, this light, the oblique angle and the gold of summer in it, allowed them to pretend they were in Spain. They spoke French. Their bodies were metropolises built on water; floating prayers in bottles bumping in a sea whose vastness left them dumb. They went everywhere glued to each other's minds and hands. When they danced at parties thrown by his friends they were like a single fuse turning in the dark. Bea introduced Cosgrove to her family.

It happened that all members of her family were present for this introduction except Duncan. The family made stern if secretive judges, but Cosgrove was an instant hit, the first of any of her men to succeed. Afterwards she and he went driving in the country, through grain fields pouring down silver to creeks, eating green miles in Bea's ancient blue car. They talked nonstop, wreathed in Gitane smoke, the skin of a melon they'd eaten glowing on the dashboard like some translucent emerald-veined womb; once Bea loosened his cock laughing, took it into her mouth as he drove, Gitane smoke drifting up through the steering-wheel. They returned home to the farm numb, ruddy, invincible, to announce their wedding plans. Without actually trying to they had arrived at a tacit understanding that the institution of marriage, though presently cliché and degraded, would be re-invented by them.

By phone from the other side of the continent Duncan got upset. Whatever Bea thought, he said, wild to change her mind at a distance of five thousand miles, she was being duped. Whatever she and this guy believed of marriage, they were wrong. By this point Duncan had been married and divorced and he was using this, Bea thought, to unfair advantage. Duncan pressed his point. Bea didn't know men like he did, Duncan said. *He was* one. "I haven't met this Cosgrove," said Duncan, "but whoever he is I don't like him. How long have you known him? How can he let you make this mistake? I don't like it. I want you to know I don't like any of it. I want to go on record: 'Duncan told Bea she was making a mistake.'" He hung up, intoning in a way that negated any flattery in the remark: "He can't possibly be good enough for you." Bea laughed. He had not hung up before telling her enthusiastically and in detail about a girl ten years his junior who was going to save his life.

Two months before the wedding, citing dreamlike personal events and Bea's tendency to break glass when overwhelmed, Cosgrove told her he couldn't go through with it. He sat on the edge of the bed stroking her cheek. He was exquisitely gentle, the pressure of skin on skin quieted her until it became the rhythm of her sleep. This was the moment Bea knew would erase death if she ever remembered it at such a time:

Cosgrove's long beautiful hand on her face, stroking it over and over, while she dreamt, half asleep, exhausted by tears, that kindness was the most she should ever have asked out of life; and the dream ending just as the door closed behind him.

Cosgrove left her, his unassailable hopefulness intact, and the last remaining outbuilding of Bea's own dangerous hopefulness caught fire. It burnt to the ground. Bea, at last, had surpassed Duncan. She had come to resemble everyone else.

When the pieces were all collected again, her chest re-fired to hold its burden of scars, Bea, age 28, realized that she would never fall in love again and never wanted to. A human being, any human being, herself included, was a compendium of facts no-one else wanted to hear. Sometimes you opened and thumbed each other's books. You swooned at the smell off the pages. Then you snapped the book shut again, lest you really start reading. Bea, like anyone else, she supposed, was now sometimes a good lover, and sometimes not. She no longer had to kiss her own arm if she didn't want to. She moved with ease in the abysses of anyone's heart, and none of it, she decided, held any possible remaining attraction. She accepted that all love is the story of audience and magician, the price of a ticket no less than her life, and turning her head from all that dazzle she had come out of the orchestra-pit into the light.

*The light there proved to be only the light of centre stage. Bea had no next love. She had two.

Frederick

Time stopped when the cicada sang. Bea's hand on the sheer curtain; the green light that came through the ivy dappling her wrist and the scar there. She could hear Frederick's voice down in the yard, husky from cigarettes and whiskey. Frederick's voice paused too, hung on the summer air like a wing. The cicada broke and the wing stooped, a soft soft glide into the grass.

Frederick was talking to Mrs. Chambers, Bea's mother. Bea was perched on the toilet-lid in the big upstairs bathroom at the farm. She still went there sometimes. The dappling green sunlight, the faintly wafting curtains, the tiled silence, settled her. Coincidentally it was also a place from which you could hear everything happening down on the drive, by the side gardens, or in the yard. Now Frederick was talking to Mrs. Chambers. Bea didn't try to make out the words, but she noticed her mother's tone of controlled grief. In a different way she noticed Freddy's tone, which never varied. He could say anything, be crude or impeccably polite, and Bea would understand the words second, if at all. His voice to her always suggested soft dark things, like his flat-fingered hands, like his eyelids that drooped at the corners. They had both inherited these eyelids from their grandfather, Bea through her mother, Freddy through his father. To Bea her own were fiercely ugly while Frederick's, when his algae-coloured eyes found her across a room, made her chest spill over, gently, terribly. In the end that was what Freddy always suggested: in the soft dark, a torrent; the beginning of a Niagara of the senses.

Bea let the curtain drop.

It was all because of their grandmother. Mrs. Chambers had gone into their grandmother's apartment one day to find her wandering and blank, a confused wrinkled child. Their grandmother could not remember if she had been to bed, could not find her glasses– even with which she was almost blind– did not seem to have eaten for a long time, was not sure who it was that had just walked in her door. Mrs. Chambers came to Bea in the living-room at the farm. "What will I do?" she sobbed. "*She didn't know me.*" Bea, who was eighteen, held her mother in her arms and for the first time felt the fierce protective love of a parent for a child. It filled her with pride. She believed herself seven feet tall and ageless. "I'll go live with her," said Bea.

Her grandmother's apartment in town was soft blue and warm but by the end it had become for Bea a high white cage of glass and light. The tips of the maples two streets over seemed so heavy with greenery Bea felt glutted looking at them, her breasts aching unbearably, mysteriously, in response: behind her inside the apartment her grandmother grew progressively smaller, more shrivelled, more quizzical. The grandmother would spend her days searching for her purse, with a blind groping motion along the edges of furniture. "Have you seen my purse?" she would ask Bea. "I seem to have lost it."

At first Bea would join in, finally locating the black pouch beside the toilet, on a shelf in the linen closet. "I'm putting it on your bedside table, okay Gramma?" she'd say. She'd take her grandmother's fragile blue-veined hand firmly and lead her to the table to see. "It's right there. Why don't you leave it there now?"

"Oh, you're such a dear," her grandmother would say, blinking in a benign way she had. "I'll do that." But she wouldn't. While Bea was reading she would move the purse again and then forget. Her small blind hunt, the punishing anxiety, were a ritual that drove her; her existence depended on the endless misplacement of something both trivial and necessary. While she groped she was living; while she rested on the brief plateau of relief she was feeling what she could of joy. To Bea this relief was most terrible of all. Its brevity made it bleak: the single breath of a relaxing Sisyphus at the top of the hill.

Later Bea refused to join the hunt. Its punishment and anxiety had become hers too. Instead she would sit her grandmother in a chair and read her things she imagined might help a human being fumbling towards death: Kahlil Gibran, W.B. Yeats. The words seemed soft and striving and comforted Bea, at least. But they became like everything else somehow infected with bleakness. Her grandmother would get up in the middle of them to find a nail file.

Meals were a similar ordeal. Bea believed that when her patience became perfect, her grandmother would finally eat. But it was like trying to force-feed a wild bird. No food could comfort what ailed her. The day Bea finally saw that she could do no more, that her grandmother would totter in her own way towards an increasingly ignominious decay, the walls of the apartment transformed suddenly to light. Air blew unbearably clean from room to room, there was no such thing as skin and Bea knew herself finally to be like her grandmother, disembodied. Her eighteen-year-old self had flooded out of her into the greening tops of the maples long ago, they were creatures of light and space who made no sense: their only hope of escape from repetition was death. It was noon. Her grandmother turned to her from a doorway, her eyes like blurred hare-bells, and said distinctly: "Whatever happened to Beatrix? She never visits me any more."

That afternoon Bea brooded, with the fierce seriousness of eighteen, over the idea of poisoning her grandmother. But in the end, regretting only that she would depart a virgin, she slit her own wrists instead.

She did it clumsily, the apartment neat as a pin around her, her grandmother tucked up for a nap, her elbows tied off with her grandfather's old neckties. Kneeling on the bathroom tiles as if in a private chapel she seemed to herself a figure on a screen devoid of pathos. But Death, the black wave she'd imagined, did not appear. Not for Bea; not for her grandmother. Instead they stitched up Bea's wrists and moved her grandmother into the loft above the garage at the farm. When the family heard how the grandmother was ailing, the gentler ones, who could still care about someone old and crazy and no longer familiar, came to visit. No-one heard about Bea. Bea wandered the farmhouse with a dark secret passion in the pit of her stomach. She did not know its object. Although she was driven to a psychiatrist once a week she said nothing; nothing of any consequence was said to her. She began to realize that through her actions she had become an embarrassment.

Around her the farm burst into high spring. Her skin remained a stranger she met only under the sough of apple-blossom in the wet night, against the bark of the pear-tree. Driven unaccountably she would embrace the trunk as if it could remove the ache in her forearms, between her legs, in her head and heart. The relatives who arrived to visit her grandmother left again one by one. When they had all been gone for some time and summer had descended on the farm in a green tide, Frederick came.

There were certain things Bea would always remember. She was wearing a pale blue shirt with long sleeves. (She still had to wear long sleeves. She'd tried not to once, convinced no-one actually looked at her closely enough to notice her discoloured forearms, and Dr. Chambers had said to her abruptly, gesturing at his own wrists for emphasis: "Are you trying to advertise?" Bea, silent, flooded with horror. She didn't wear short sleeves again until the following summer.) She was perched on the counter alone in the kitchen. The curtains had been drawn for coolness; it was a bright warm day. Light flooded out of the summer-porch in a gold glow through the sliding screen door and Bea was swinging her feet into and out of it. Her feet were bare. She was wearing a favourite pair of baggy white pants which stood in great disfavour with her parents on account of their bagginess. Bea, who considered herself fat, loved them. She looked up from her feet. Her long hair was cut with bangs that fell into her eyes; she had to shake them back to look beyond the table and the pass-through into the old play-room. Through the picture window there the fields and woods shimmered in the heat; where the garden drooped around the bird-bath the peony heads made pink splashes above soil still dark from a night shower. The humidity was intense. Bea's eyes drew back into the house, to a photograph sitting on the pass-through. In it her mother, wearing a fur hat and collar, turned with a half smile from a hedge gleaming with hoar frost. One small gloved hand rested on the latch of a snow-lipped picket fence; she held a branch of wild cranberry over one shoulder. In this picture Mrs. Chambers was thirteen, but her face– in structure rather than content– might have been that of someone thirty-five. Bea marked the greys of sky, the particular light on her mother's turned, suddenly-caught face, the breath misting in the air above the fence; she believed intensely in their existence. For a moment suddenly she was there: both with her mother and behind the camera, alive in the snowy day, her own breath catching from cold in her lungs, the exact sunlight sparking from the frosted hedge, her mother, a child, lifting her red mouth in a grin. Then Bea was back again, her usual self sitting in her blue blouse on the counter, her wrists aching because her fists were clenched. Her head felt dazzled from having disappeared and reappeared so quickly. While she sat marvelling, the back doorbell rang.

The ring at the door would be Frederick's brother Nicholas, who lived nearby and had promised to call. Nicholas was the same age as Bea's oldest brother and she didn't think about him much; he'd once been known for his questionable table manners, a flaw he'd grown out of but not lost the reputation for. She hopped off the counter, went into the front hall and yelled up to her mother that Nick had come. Then she padded out through the flagstone entry and carelessly, if shyly, opened the back door. There was Frederick.

Time skipped a beat while she replaced the fat and vaguely formless Freddy of five years ago with the brown stranger sprung up in their doorway. He had chestnut curls and green eyes which filled instantly with astonishment. Bea, who was plagued by a habit of seeing unspoken things without knowing her place in them, watched a mask fall immediately and irretrievably from Frederick's face. The mask broke on the step between them, where it lay now ignored; and in the second before Bea turned to greet Nick, standing to one side, she knew, certainly and for once, that somehow it was she in whose honour the mask had fallen. The knowledge made her intensely, secretly glad. Had her face been less white, her bangs properly trimmed, her pants well-fitting, her shirt short-sleeved, the look on her face kinder or less desperate, it might never have happened. When she turned from Nick and embraced Freddy, a polite cousin, he stood stiffly, still staring. She led them into the house.

From then on Freddy's eyes never left her. She was too confused to look but she felt them, like a green heat laid over and over against her skin. She avoided him carefully and wondered what to do. Because she had decided instantly, begun to believe with something approaching religious passion, that somehow Freddy's mask had fallen in recognition of her own, smashed in their grandmother's bathroom, and that now he was the only one who could heal her.

Much later Bea crept away to draw in her room. Sketching released her from inarticulateness. A whole day's humiliations would skate smooth on the line of her pencil. The lines became her talisman against failure; on paper her general terror of life transmuted to a pure energy fearsome in its intensity, and skirled there in lead another Bea rose up for her like a chant. The chant consoled her, told her that some day she would matter because of this, someday this would give her strengths she didn't yet know how to harness. Some day also the psychiatrist who sat silent and contemptuous of her shyness, sucking his unlit pipe, would see with shame that he had been blind and pompous; some day Dr. Chambers would understand how bitterly the long bruises on her wrists still bled inside her heart. Some day Mrs. Chambers would realize that her sociable solutions to Bea's condition were unutterably beside the point. When Bea drew she was seeing for them all, for her parents and the psychiatrist and her brothers and her grandmother, preparing them all for some day– it never came, though it remained in her imagination always immanent– when everything fell apart, the common appearance of things folded, and whatever held life together until then stepped forward revealed to judge them. It was a day that Bea had always foreseen, always understood would come, without ever wanting to. Bea's longing to be blind and dumb empowered the fantastical, the radiant, and the obsessive, which bloomed under her fist in the green sketch-book.

Bea tried to draw Freddy. Somehow he became her mother. She was drawing her mother as she was now, turned under the old frosted hedge from the photograph but with flowers over her shoulder. The flowers folded back and back, more flowers and more flowers, flowers within flowers– Bea had just decided this, begun to make them burgeon fiercely under her pencil, when she knew that Frederick was standing in the door behind her. She froze. Then, breathless that he might look at the pictures which no-one had ever seen before, breathless that he might fail to look, she went on drawing. The flowers rioted; the winter hedge bloomed; Freddy stood by her shoulder and bending his head close to her own said softly: "So which one is me?"

Bea's sullen heart turned over painfully. She lifted her pencil as he came round to sit on the twin bed looking at her.

"Beatrix."

"Yes?"

"Send me drawings? Send me some, while I'm gone?"

Freddy was an agriculture consultant. On what grounds no-one had been able to figure out, but it seemed largely personal charm and a knack for teaching things. Certainly, at 29, it was felt it could not be experience. Right now he was on his way to three months in Africa where he intended to help a tiny local government carve farms out of jungle.

"Bea? Will you?"

Frederick's slow eyes fell directly onto her soul and her soul lay naked there, arms out, wrists upturned, drowning before his gaze. He smiled: a deep, heavy-lidded, liquid smile.

Bea's pre-Raphaelite period began. She covered her bedroom walls with posters. King Cophetua gazed down from his throne, incalculably worldly, upon the wan averted face of the beggar-maid. Waterhouse's dead Ophelia drifted, rimed with flowers, wreathed in her brocade dress, down an emerald stream. Bea found something ultimately stiff and terrible about the dead Ophelia, and after a while she took that picture down. Later she read that the young prostitute who modelled for Waterhouse, lying motionless in soaked drapes in a cold copper tub, had died of pneumonia. Later still she read that the faces of Burne-Jones' towering women, the dark stare of Rossetti's Persephone were not someone seen in a fever but portraits of Jane Morris who, although married to William, secretly bedded his friends. But there were two pictures she loved. One was the Lady of Shallot at the centre of a burst tapestry, her black hair electric while in the mirror Lancelot rode away slothful and carefree. The other was Burne-Jones' *The Beguiling of Merlin*. Bea would look at this as she drew her pictures for Freddy and ache for a Merlin of her own undone with just such desire and love. She imagined Freddy, languishing gracefully before her. She barely asked herself what came next, what she would do with Freddy as he languished there. She stared at the snuffed coals of Merlin's eyes and dreamt on.

Later she could admit that she had seduced Freddy with her pencil as surely, with as much curiosity and negligence, as that with which Merlin's nemesis glanced over the page of her incantation. But for now life withheld its motive; there were things that, if Bea had known them, might have prevented her from doing anything at all.

He sent her one postcard, an aerial view of jungle. On it he'd made a few doodles meant as pictographs of two smiling faces—one with a pencil stuck in its hair (Bea); one being menaced by a pencil (Freddy). In a cryptic line he explained that her drawings were too beautiful. They intimidated him so he couldn't write back.

Secretly Bea found something disappointing in this answer. As if to make up for his delinquency she never wavered. She sent him eighteen more pages of drawings. When he had been gone six weeks she stopped, because he had suddenly reappeared.

There was some scandal around Freddy's abrupt reappearance which Mrs. Chambers looked grim about and Bea didn't hear first-hand. But she was given to understand Freddy's contract had been terminated early because he drank. He had been demoted (although it was never discussed in these terms). He was sent to work in the fields of an agricultural experiment station twenty miles from the Chambers' farm. Bea only learned this when her parents talked around it at dinner. She felt slighted that Freddy had not informed her himself, but her interest picked up.

"Does Nick know for sure that was the whole story?" Dr. Chambers was asking sceptically.

Mrs. Chambers said: "With Frederick, who knows?"

Dr. Chambers, peering out the long picture-window at the wind running in the barley fields, said grimly, not with much hope but with great satisfaction: "I hope this teaches him a lesson."

Mrs. Chambers went to pour tea. "We can only hope," she said, with sympathy because it was her brother's son, but with no more conviction. Bea left the table and sat on the side steps to drink her tea. Sun glanced off the new apples in the orchard.

A week later Bea came in from swimming at the pond to find Freddy in the kitchen. He was talking to his aunt as smoothly, as winningly, as a favoured nephew with a hundred successes behind him. Freddy looked at Bea; his face lit and his eyes went half asleep. Bea had grown a little thinner, from not trying to, and it gave her confidence. She flushed.

Freddy asked Bea to show him the pond. Mrs. Chambers

shooed them out, covering her palpable misgivings with her own show of the indulgent aunt. He told Bea as they took the track to the pond that all his life he'd thought Claudine Chambers one of the most beautiful women he'd ever seen. He had, he said, boasted about his aunt to friends; how she looked as refined and genteel as their grandfather, how she never seemed to age. He lifted his face to the sunset, letting the barley tassels slip across the tips of his brown fingers. Bea, watching his fingers and the barley, felt the blood rush to her feet. Freddy said nothing about her. Bea noted this, but took herself, in the context of his other admirations– the field, her mother– to be flattered. Everyone said that Bea and Mrs. Chambers looked remarkably alike.

They stood on the bank of the pond where Liam's ducks, put out for summer, patrolled for scraps. Bea always travelled with a pocketful of oats and she threw it to them while she and Freddy stood wordless in the smell of purple vetch. A late bumble-bee buzzed somewhere. Bea, nervous and excited, felt her being contract to a point. "Sh!" she whispered suddenly. "Close your eyes." She did. "Listen." She stood hushed and taut. "Do you hear them? The ducks eating? It sounds like water babbling over stones." They waited. Dew had begun at Bea's bare feet and ankles, the crickets sang, a last robin called from a maple tree. The ducks' bills gabbled in the water, snapping up grain. In the waiting dusk they saw a stream appear at their feet. Or Bea saw that. "Do you hear it?"

"Bea... "

She turned, opened her eyes. She smiled. She could just see Freddy's eyes, luminous against a sky gone ink. His hand lifted and fell again. Something crackled. Bea swung away, embarrassed. They strolled back up to the house talking softly of their love for plants, inherited from both their grandparents. Bea told him about their grandmother: wandering out of the house, poking her finger into the garden soil, whispering kindly to an explosion of irises: "Oh, you could do with a drink."

She looked out her window as the sun fell behind the house.

She had been to see the psychiatrist. He'd sat still, looking at her. He had waited. Overwhelmed by her need to cross the humiliating silence she told him how, at noon, she had stood in the pond staring up at the sky while a white glider soared across its blueness. Lower down a gull wheeled, back and forth across the glider's invisible path.

"I had this idea," Bea told him shyly, "of how quiet and peaceful it must be up there. I wished I was in that glider. Somehow. If I could be."

The psychiatrist sat unmoving for a long time. Finally he stirred and knocked out his pipe.

"Well," he said. "What did you want to discuss today?"

From her bedroom window Bea looked out at the pear trees and the barley field and curled her wrists into the crooks of her elbows. Behind the house it seemed that Death, the betraying wave who had beckoned but never taken her hand, was going away forever. She took off her clothes and crawled through her window onto the roof. She climbed the peak of the garage under which her grandmother slept with unfathomable dreams and stood on the ridge naked, staring at the retreated sun. She understood that the flush of shame bared on her skin might never recede. She began to shake. In her chest something broke from the chill of the psychiatrist's words. Misery spilled out of her, his gift to her for failing to find suitable words of her own. She saw only uselessness in the green sketchbook closed under her pillow. It began to rain softly. She stood there for a long time while the horizon faded from crimson to gold and snuffed out. Tears joined the rain on her bare feet and ran onto the shingles.

Next evening they stood on the bank of the pond. They were restless. Bea couldn't think of any stories about their grandmother and Freddy smacked at the weeds with a stick. Then suddenly he said: "Bea sometimes, if we weren't cousins ..." and fell silent again. Bea waited. When he didn't go on she saw for the first time that what she considered inevitable might never happen. She turned to him. "What does it matter if we're cousins?" she said. "Artists don't care. They should experience everything." She felt that this might sound ridiculous, but it was all she could think of. Everything she knew concentrated on his response. Freddy blinked once and put his arms around her. They stood lightly encircled staring out at the water while Bea's heart pounded with elation and terror. She shut out the future. Words tumbled in her throat. She was trembling.

"You knew, didn't you?" she said. "About my wrists?"

"What?"

"I thought you saw– " She turned her palms up and lifted her cuffs. Freddy stared. Then he sank into the grass. His arms constricted suddenly and angrily around her knees. His face pressed into her thighs. Wild carrot caught there filtered his breath across her bare skin, its crushed scent sharp on mist now fleeing off the pond. Bea's hands tightened as if they held a pencil and then expanded and when he pulled her onto her knees too her hands went instinctively to his hair. He said sadly, "Give us a kiss." Crickets shouted around them in the dark.

She struggled free of him and jumped to her feet. She ran up the honeysuckle lane that she knew leaf by leaf in the dark. He caught her at the door and when she swung they melted against the wall of the house; the house scraped the back of his hands and her arms as her flesh lilted into his palms. "Little cousin," he mocked when his head lifted. He was laughing, his soft hoarse laugh. Always after that his laugh set something in Bea spinning. "That wasn't exactly what I had in mind." But Bea didn't believe him. It seemed right to her that on this step where masks had broken an entirely different world should begin its tendril up her leg. It was a world whose advance she had long expected, whose delays had laid blades across her pulse and whose advent now became as necessary, as intricate, as astonishing, as the delicately charged sweetness of his tongue.

He took her to the ramshackle motel where he lived by a field of wild roses. As they went out they said good-bye to Mrs.

Chambers with a charge of deception crackling between them; their glances to each other when they turned on the flagstones of the back entry were full of messages not only withheld from Mrs. Chambers, but laid in the foundation of a wall against her. Mrs. Chambers had made it clear to Bea in private that she did not quite approve of Freddy (although she never elaborated). But she loved him because of blood and she believed– quixotically, Bea thought– that his friendship with Bea might do them both some good. Bea went with Freddy, the day round with sun, car windows rolled down, wind whipping in her hair. Grinning softly he caught a rope of it and wrapped it around his palm. She had no idea what her going with him might be supposed to mean, no idea which messages in the complex vernacular of sex she had set free. She knew nothing. She felt nervous but unable to let on. They sat in the sun by his paint-peeling window, at a burn-pocked arborite table, and he showed her his photographs of Africa. The scent of wild roses from the field next door blew between them across the album's sleek pages. He had been in love with Africa: the glut of jungle, fruit the size of melons, slicing, tipping their sun-warmed juice down his throat. He drank stronger things too. He smashed someone's car. Young women– children, really, 13, 14– followed after him, calling "Mister, Mister," begging for green-eyed babies. When he told Bea how that had tempted him she felt jealous and didn't know where to look. He also told her about his job. There was a grass-hut bar where he had beaten up his boss. At issue had been some point of honour: Frederick had been raised by his military father in schools that stressed a certain ruined ideal of manhood. He would never be promoted again. To all this Bea said nothing, because although the photographs flipped under her fingers she never saw them. She saw only his brown hands. She was imagining them on her body.

He noticed her silence at last. "Bea," he said. "I have to tell you something. You should be careful of me. I drink too much. I'm what you might call a womanizer."

Bea flushed deeply and did not look up from her lap. She

failed to see what this had to do with anything, with her and with him.

"So?" she said.

He brushed her bent head. Both of them, at the same time, smiled.

They drove home in the summer dark with stars wheeling over the car like lit footballs and fireflies lighting streaks in the ditches. At the last corner before the farm he pulled the car over and stopped. He came round to her door. She opened it before he could, stood up into the crush of her own receded breath. Pressed together, fireflies floating beyond them, the boundaries of their bodies began to merge under a still-approaching wave.

Later he held Bea's face between his hands and looked at her cheeks under the yard light. He leaned and bit her ear softly, laughing. "Whisker burn," he said against her hair.

In her bedroom mirror, under plain electric light she found difficult to believe in now, she stared at her bright cheeks and chin, the faint red burning around her mouth. It was the first time she had seen or heard of such a thing. She knew suddenly that she was born to it.

Frederick didn't visit for two days. Bea wandered the house in her bare feet, clutching her sketchbook but never drawing in it. Anticipation turned to dismay, then anger. She believed herself misused and neglected. She sat over lunch with Mrs. Chambers, curtains drawn against the heat, and picked at her fruit. Mrs. Chambers wanted to know what Bea intended doing next with her life. Bea was going away to school in the fall, of course; the same university Dr. and Mrs. Chambers had attended, and at which they had met. But in the meantime, what was she going to do with herself? She had to get a job. She couldn't mope around the house. She had to answer for her responsibilities. Bea tried to think what her responsibilities might be, but she couldn't imagine any. Several people whom Mrs. Chambers considered kind had offered Bea jobs, which Bea was doing her best to ignore. One she had already turned down. Mrs. Chambers poured lemonade. Her voice lifted a notch. "*Bea!*" Bea put down her fork and looked at her mother. All she could register was that this same person had sat with her in the psychiatrist's office that first day and said to him sincerely: "Whatever Beatrix wants. If she needs a summer just to relax in the sun at the pond, that's fine with us."

"I'm going to draw," Bea said to her mother suddenly. "I decided last night. I'm really happy about it. I don't want those jobs, because I'm going to work on my art and take it seriously."

Mrs. Chambers listened to this tolerantly. "That's fine," she said. "But dear, drawing is a lonely pursuit. You've got to stop spending so much time alone. You've got to learn to be more active and involved."

In those days this was Mrs. Chambers' favourite angle of argument with Bea. *Push yourself,* she was fond of saying. She grew concerned whenever she felt Bea's shyness was showing. Mrs. Chambers seemed to champion a life which, however elegantly lived, was lived with more determination than enjoyment. Bea hated the idea. Unknown to all of them, including Bea herself, Bea was a hedonist at heart. She sat dully, listening to her mother, and saw the same old impasse stretch out between them. For her mother Bea's only problem lay in not being an extrovert like herself.

"*Mum,*" Bea said. "I'm *serious*. It *matters* to me."

"Bea, you need a job. We expect you to help pay for school."

"I don't want to go there anyway," Bea retorted, which was a surprise to both of them, and then the front doorbell rang. Its chimes cut across her mother's reply. "Will you get that please?" Mrs. Chambers added. The subject of Bea was one Mrs. Chambers could only deal with in short spurts. Much later Bea understood that what tired her mother out was a belief in her own guilt for all that Bea had failed to become. Bea padded through the front hall.

It was Frederick. Two more days of work in the fields had darkened him, streaked his curls, soaked light into his moss-coloured eyes. He was holding a bunch of ditch weeds. Purple vetch, daisies and Indian paintbrush cascaded out of his fist onto his arm. As usual whenever he first saw Bea on the other side of a door, he looked astonished.

They didn't greet each other. "Will you marry me?" he whispered. He stood very still looking at her. Gradually Bea realized that he was waiting for an answer, that Freddy, twelve years older than her, would only ask this question seriously. She felt proud and alarmed. He waited. Faintly aware of doing some great violence, too inexperienced to avoid it, she laughed carelessly up at him as if he had made a flattering joke and didn't answer at all. "Who is it dear?" Mrs. Chambers called from the kitchen.

"Freddy."

Without smiling Freddy lowered his mouth to Bea's throat.

"Come on in then you two!" Mrs. Chambers called gaily. They went in, decorous, and presented her with the flowers.

When they could escape to the orchard Bea turned on him. "You said you'd come and you didn't," she said. "I've been waiting for *two days*."

"Bea, I came when I could. We're on extended hours. I'm already skipping out as it is, I'm probably going to lose even *this* job."

"You *said* you'd come."

"Beatrix don't make me angry."

They looked at each other, stricken. "Do you know what?" he said softly. "I don' t even care if I lose it."

Bea took his hand. She laced her tongue over his thumb, around his fingers until he pushed her against a trunk. They stood unbearably still. Somehow up till now Freddy had always been circumspect with her ignorance but now his penis, grown insistent and unfamiliar under his clothes, was a new presence pressed between them. Shocked, Bea looked up at him. In Freddy's eyes were the beginnings of a besottedness so deep it frightened her. Lifting her hands swiftly she covered them. He

81

only pressed his eyes into her palms.

"I shaved," he said. "For you."

The blue spruce stood in the open lower lawn like a musty ghost, swallows diving around it. In the orchard the apples of the first tree to ripen blushed between the leaves. Occasionally one fell with a dull thud into the grass where the smell of bruised fruit made a sweet skirt round the trunk. Iris Mrs. Chambers had transplanted from her parents' farm after her father died stood beside the patio tipped with dark wilted tatters of bloom. Their lingering smell of licorice floated past the steps.

Bea and Frederick sat with their grandmother under the oldest tree in the orchard. Its gnarled hollows supported countless families of sparrows. They sat on an old park bench which Dr. Chambers had rescued from some city junk heap; between them their grandmother raised her frail face as if to feel the tree's dappled sun and shadow. She was blind, but her hearing and her sense of smell were sharp. She registered the smells and birdsong and they played over her features in waves.

Bea was sketching. She had stopped drawing fantastical things abruptly and without regret. Now she sketched her grandmother as if she would make herself remember forever: the fine nose molded at the nostrils, the wide cheekbones, the large clouded eyes. Deep, contemplative shadows offset the eyes of everyone in the grandmother's family. Bea's father, travelling west to meet Mrs. Chambers' relatives, had confessed to an eerie feeling as familiar, grave eyes of a particularly piercing blue appeared in unknown face after unknown face stepping out of prairie houses. A robin called somewhere. Bea drew her grandmother whole, frail, and elemental as she sat, absorbed into the elements of air, dollops of shadow rustling on her cheekbones and back and forth over one fine, skinny hand. The other hand lay in Frederick's. Bea drew that, too: their grandmother's silken bones across Frederick's young strong brown ones.

Their grandmother spoke. "It's good of you to come and visit me," she said happily. "You must come more often and next time we'll all go for a drive." Frederick and Bea looked at each other over their grandmother's head. Tears brimmed in Freddy's eyes. Bea smiled. She drew them all, Frederick weeping silently, their grandmother calm with a blind person's unspeakable joys, her own head bent over the pencil. She dropped the pencil and flung her arms around her grandmother.

"Thank you Gramma!" Bea cried.

"What for dear?"

"Without you, we wouldn't be here."

"Oh, aren't you sweet," their grandmother responded gravely.

The grandmother's presence at the farm, her rustling through rooms, feeling along cushions for her lost purse, her small high insistent voice calling "Claudine, Claudine," like a baby bird waiting to be fed, had begun to take its toll on Mrs. Chambers. Her temper had grown shorter and now erupted over small things. The dark circles under her eyes darkened more. A harassed looked carved itself into her forehead, around her mouth. She would cry at imagined slights: if Dr. Chambers mentioned leftovers in the fridge, if Liam forgot to introduce his friends, if Bea refused meat at dinner, if Jeffrey, who was chronically late for everything, missed his weekend train from the city.

Bea's other brothers and their wives were aware of the change in Claudine Chambers. Family gatherings and Sunday suppers began to include secret conferences– by the shed, in the side garden, watching horses in the paddock, walking through the woods– about the state of their mother's nerves. Small strategies were hatched by the sisters-in-law to keep Mrs. Chambers as cushioned from her own condition as possible; explanations about their gramma and great-gramma were made to children. But the nieces and nephews had an innate respect for madness. Better than anyone they understood the vicissitudes, not only of the old, but of life for those who stayed by them. For the children, as for Dr. and Mrs. Chambers, the idea of putting the grand-mother in a home belonged to the realm of the inconceivable, like sending her to Mars. "It's not what she is now," Mrs. Chambers had told Bea once, "it's what she was. She doesn't *deserve* any less." This was the dignity that made Bea love her mother. It was a dignity the children, to everyone's faint surprise, considered natural.

The brothers and sisters-in-law whispered on, resolving their distress with explanations and jokes, or they gathered strength by airing questions about Claudine Chambers' brothers, who grieved at a distance, their mother's decay too upsetting to them to visit often. Then one by one they would drift into the room where the grandmother sat at such gatherings ensconced in a blue-and-white knitted blanket. They would greet and kiss her; they would lap briefly at the reward of the bright, reflexive smile she never lost. Then loving her, and seeing in their minds' eyes the lines on their mother's face, they would wish death on their grandmother. All waited for it now: the loss which would also release them. Death had softened, lost its dark niche Bea had imagined hers alone, and become a deliverer they all waited for, the only one who could relieve their mother of this grief so that the real, the final, grieving could begin.

Meanwhile to lift the strain and take her mother's mind off the life she still expected Bea at any time to embark on, Bea had begun taking more duties with the grandmother.

At first Dr. Chambers frowned on this. He- and the colleague who had stitched Bea up- saw a logical connection between the mad old woman and Bea's defaced wrists. Once, before Frederick came, Dr. Chambers had found Bea sitting on the front stairs. "How are you feeling?" he'd asked her carefully. Behind his inscrutable doctor's manner Bea saw a trembling confusion. She wrapped her arms around herself. She felt she was addressing a small boy who had asked to have the secrets of the universe explained. She was the only one who knew that there was no explanation. "I feel sick to my stomach all the time," she told him.

"You do." He nodded. It was a confirmation, not a question.

His shoulders slumped. He went on out to the patio, where Bea heard him say to Mrs. Chambers: "An eighteen-year-old is no match for an eighty-six-year-old. We should have known." In that moment, Bea loved him as much as she ever had.

But the grandmother never went away. When her mother's face seemed unlikely to bear any more strain, Bea would take her grandmother for long walks. The tension between the three of them remained as thick as summer humidity. Only at Frederick's arrival would her mother's forehead unfurl. Frederick dropped into the warp of their lives as smoothly as a stone. Nothing Bea did, however much she wanted it, had the same effect. She began to accept this as typical of love: whatever you sent out, something always came back– from a different direction, or glancing wide of its mark.

Usually Frederick came on these walks with them. Once past the barn he would gather Bea into his arms as if he would absorb her limbs and hair. Bea grew used to the sweet dull press of his groin, the weight of his body, where on his throat she could smooth her mouth until he gasped. She moved from alarm to fascination to longing while their grandmother tottered in the lane with her face to the sun or bent sometimes to test the ground for moisture, muttering to the grass. The wave that stooped over them redolent with summer curved closer and closer until it had touched the ground beyond and they stood alone under it, they and their grandmother, oblivious in a glimmer of weeds and skin.

Still Bea's timidity was greater than her need. In his own way Frederick became patient– or she believed he did. Much later she understood that Frederick had a deep, an abiding, failure of confidence in himself, and that was why– eclipsing skin and eyes and genes– he loved her: he loved in Bea the same frightened soul he knew inside himself.

Sometimes they remembered they were first cousins. Then they would rehearse to themselves that they were *related*, that their parents were *brother and sister*, mining their embraces for potential shock-value with the family. *What if your dad came out now, What if YOUR dad– What if Nicholas, Aunt Nellie wouldn't mind–* ... Sometimes Frederick evoked for them both cloudy images of a Victorian past when people regularly married their cousins, and they would ponder the mystery of misplaced Time with bemusement and regret. Eventually they learned to bandy the word "incest" between them with racy grins and no hint of guilt. But somewhere sadder and deeper it still owned them– owned Freddy, the older and more responsible, most of all.

Then Frederick lost his job. There were too many nights spent grappling in the dusk. He was fired for coming late.

The day he came to tell Bea he was ecstatic; he lifted her into the air and swung her round and tumbled her into the grass carelessly, in full view of the house. He began to make himself indispensable around the farm. He helped Jeffrey and Liam and Dr. Chambers with the haying, he showed up in the kitchen with baskets of cherries or plums, he took their grandmother for drives, fed her, walked with her in the gardens reciting the names of flowers. She now saw them only as blotches of colour but they had all once come from her own gardens and she would brighten as if greeting friends. Freddy sat over coffee with his aunt telling sly jokes in his whiskey voice until she laughed. Once Bea came in from feeding the horses to find her mother's tired head bowed, her eyes closed, and Freddy massaging her shoulders. Freddy looked up at Bea over her mother's bent neck. He gave her his smile perpetually heavy with suggestion. The rhythm of his hands changed. Their touch on her mother's neck rang through Bea's body.

As company for Bea, Liam was undependable and Jeffrey was boarding at his job in the city. So it was because of Frederick that Dr. and Mrs. Chambers felt able to take a trip. The trip was Dr. Chambers' idea. With Freddy around, his concerns about the grandmother's effect on Bea had faded. He persuaded Bea's mother to spend four days at a friend's cottage. They called it their "romantic weekend," laughing: it was a curious characteristic of the Chambers that while they loved each other with a certain openness and warmth, they disapproved of similar behaviour in the young, and above all in the unmarried. This meant that Liam, who had grown into a lanky, laconic youth, unbiddable by anyone, had taken to cars and parties to roll his girls while Bea, eager to please, less naturally a rebel, was left alone in her parents' uneasy fortress of circumscribed sensuality. Bea had come vaguely to understand the thing which had leapt between her and Freddy on the doorstep. It had been the moment of recognition between a pillager and his prize. Bea was her parents' bored treasure, and Freddy was the thief.

They stood with their grandmother on the curved front drive under the pines and waved to Dr. and Mrs. Chambers as the green car pulled away. They sat their grandmother on the porch swing. When the car turned at the corner, they kissed. Frederick's hand slipped under Bea's shirt and slid the length of her back. He drew it out again and sucked her sweat off his palm.

They fell immediately into a routine. It was as if they had been at it for years.

It was no lie that Freddy drank. He had discovered Dr. Chambers' liquor cupboard under the front staircase. He would put their grandmother to sleep, so they wouldn't have to worry about her wandering at night, by lacing her evening tea with rum. They would settle her in bed when the summer dusk was still pale and her distant blue eyes would blink once at them benignly. They would stand for a few minutes looking at her until she slept. Both saw the same thing: a mystery of bone and silver hair who had once cradled their parents. Above her on the great carved headboard of the bed, burl-maple fish-demons Bea first encountered there in childhood rushed faithfully towards all threats.

Then they'd go downstairs and Freddy would pour himself a scotch. Bea preferred wine. Glasses and decanters in hand they sat together on the wicker couch as evening cooled in the summer-porch. Liam occasionally wandered through the kitchen, sometimes with a silent brown-eyed girl, sometimes alone, drawing on a bottle and belching genially as he passed.

Liam was the only one at the farm who knew about Bea and Freddy. They honoured him by making no effort to dissemble; he honoured them with his sidelong indulgent grin. It shamed Bea faintly but it also comforted her. Strangely, most of the family agreed that Liam, age 15, was a person whose good opinion meant something. For Bea he was all that she longed to be: independent, sufficient, sensual, a social success, and lived close enough to the world of his teenage peers– something Bea had never done– to be constantly on the edge of trouble. He bore the distinction of heading the local OPPs' private list of teenagers remarkable for the parties they threw, one of a core of young and hospitable Lotharios heaving cases of beer, entertaining girls with carefully curled hair and tight jeans, while they passed around joints in the light of bonfires or the high beams of their lovingly souped-up, second-hand cars. The regard of such a truant, at least to Bea, was worth something.

The night before the Chambers' return they'd spent the dusk gathering flowers to fill the house. Mock orange, pansies, roses and peonies, zinnias and wild carrot rioted from bowls and vases on every surface or littered their petals over the floor.

"It's strange," Freddy murmured. "I feel as if we've been living together for years."

Both of them were silent for a moment. They seemed to look down a long corridor of time: it had never existed, yet they recognized its curves as if they had shared it all. Bea glanced at Freddy. Unfamiliar lines ran down his brown cheeks, through his evening stubble. She saw for the first and last time that he had loved her much longer and better than she would ever understand; that just as she lost herself carefully, fearfully, in a sea of feeling he had been treading there forever, beating the waves with faltering strokes, waiting for her to join him.

"Bea," said Frederick, "will you ever sleep with me?"

Only sleep, he said later. Tonight. He held her hand as they sat on the floor of the summer-porch leaning against the wicker couch. Her heart and ears and throat were full of soft insinuations from his eyes, his words, the smell of whiskey. He had long ago quit smoking so that she wouldn't taste it in his kisses. He returned to a mango he was cutting. He had bought it for her because she'd never seen one. Now he cut it above her bare knees, the smell coming sharp and wild. Juice ran down his wrist. "Bea," he said. "Please."

He held out the piece of mango. When she took it he bent and licked the juice from her knee. His mouth lingered and moved up her thigh. The porch misted into the dark. He blurred with the taste of mango, peaches and pine sap mixed together, curls and mouth alive in her lap. The kitchen clock ticked towards midnight. "Freddy," Bea whispered. "Freddy– "

"All right," she said.

He raised his head. "Pardon?"

"I said yes."

He smiled: his soft, slow, torrential smile.

In the end she had to overcome her final misgivings by asking Liam. Liam wandered into the summer porch smirking and sucking gently at his beer-bottle. Did he mind about– them sleeping together?

Liam leaned against the doorjamb and scratched his bare chest. He looked lazily from one to the other. His eyes drooped at the corners too and she saw in her brother the familiar ghost: she, Freddy, Liam, Mrs. Chambers, their grandfather, Nicholas, their other brothers, Freddy's father and their other uncles. Where they'd always stood separate, their connections and boundaries a matter of implacable assumption, she now stood with Freddy removed from the last polite space, testing connection, blood, as boundaries thinned and parted.

"Nah," said Liam, and tilted his beer.

The one duty they'd given Liam– mostly to ensure he came home at night– was to check on their grandmother before he went to bed. Tonight they left him and parted to get ready. Frederick had promised to wear pyjama bottoms. He was careful to make her understand the great gallantry of this gesture— usually he wore nothing. Bea herself elected to wear a pair of pyjamas that had once been her grandfather's. She had appropriated them— as she appropriated most clothes, especially, to her parents' continual disappointment, if they were used or eccentric— because they were forty years old and made of striped black silk. She drew them on, whispering over her hips, trembling a little, and began to brush her hair. Tonight Liam had gone to check on their grandmother unaccountably early and Bea began to wonder if he was discreetly absenting himself. She had already fumbled the hairbrush twice and caught it again when her door creaked.

She froze, brush poised to descend. In the second before she turned she had already taken in Liam's white face, his absolute stillness. It was a stillness Bea had seen on Liam only once before, in the hospital when he was very ill. She dropped the brush. "Bea— " he said but she was past him, flying down the front staircase, to her own shock inarticulate cries stumbling over each other in her throat as her knees nearly buckled at the bottom step of the flight to her grandmother's room. "Gramma?" she called, one foot on the stair. The sound of her voice had to her ears an echo she'd never heard, her own high familiar tones, their pitiful resonance nudging against eternity. For the first time Bea came close to fainting. But she didn't. She ascended the staircase and there was her grandmother, grey as old paper, tiny, immobile, lying on the floor, her powder-blue nightgown twisted around her legs. Her legs lay still. Her eyes were closed. Her nostrils were pinched tight and she breathed delicately with the light rapid breaths of a fleeing animal. Bea knelt and took her grandmother's face in her hands.

"Gramma. Gramma, are you all right? Can you move?"

The grandmother's head shifted. Bea looked up at Liam as he arrived at the top of the stairs. He reached for the phone.

In the endless half-hour before the ambulance came Bea and Liam sat with their grandmother. Halfway through Freddy appeared, stopped as he took them in, sat by Bea still silent, holding one of the grandmother's hands. A tear splashed onto it. Looking at him in that moment Bea understood why his father had never visited their grandmother. Her uncle's grief simply at the tenor of his mother's existence would have shattered him. Only Freddy was strong enough, young enough, to carry it. Liam clutched their grandmother's other hand, staring inarticulate at the floor. Bea had not moved from her post by her grandmother's head. They had covered her with the blue crocheted blanket but they were afraid to lift or straighten her. They had not turned on a light. Dusk had given way to night. Moths pinged softly against the screens and were gone. Stars burned through the panes. Waves of cricket-song rose lapping against the house, wafted in on gusts of night breeze and beat, beat, against the crumbled walls of their grandmother's life, of their own which had always had her in it. The pine that stooped over the garage, the banks of honeysuckle and mock orange curving below the garden, the ranked iris-spears with their clubs of seed, the orchard, heavy with fruit and slumbering bees, swelled in Bea's senses to a presence outside Time that lifted green arms as one body, arched and joined over the house, covering their grandmother's spirit from any encroaching grief. Her own grief towered as high as the risen garden, risen not in revolt but something wilder. For Bea herself revolt ran clear, through her and out; she saw her life as something finally separate from her mother's, her brother's, her father's, above all her grandmother's; in the impassioned night beating outside the house she located every met challenge of her grandmother's life and knew that she, Bea, had made or assisted none of it. Her grandmother's face showed like carved stone in yard light that fell through one window. Bea forced herself to look at it. What she saw was settling, coldness, the resignation to pain that signalled ends. She was terrified of the depth of loneliness that overwhelmed her then. She bent close to her grandmother. Laying her mouth against her cold ear she whispered *I love you Gramma, always*, feeling that this was not a thing done or said any more but she could not live if she did not say it, and in the dimness her grandmother seemed to settle a little more: all that was left her by way of a response. Then Liam leapt up because loud pounding had begun at the side door.

It was the ambulance. Freddy stared blindly at the pine tree while they took her away. Bea did not. The attendants in official-looking jackets came up the narrow stairs quickly with their intravenous bag and tube and their collapsible metal stretcher with its rubberized wheels. They checked her grandmother's pulse, her blood pressure. They reached for the twisted hem of her nightgown but with a cry Bea pulled them back and straightened it herself. They asked to feel bones. Under the alien, affronting gaze of the attendants Bea uncovered each skinny bit of her grandmother in turn, loathing its necessity, loathing herself and them for betraying her grandmother's nakedness. The attendants' hands probed her grandmother's blotched and bony shanks, the shadows between each rib, blue swelling like a tumour over one withered hip.

"Her hip's broken," they said, trying to be kind. "She's had a fall, it's the most common injury we see with old women." Their tone seemed to suggest that things would be fine, that this was routine, that they would unfurl erasure from their stretcher and i.v. hose. But Bea did not believe them. She was trapped, unable to move or speak, in a grey hospital hall where her grandmother sat half-collapsed in a wheelchair as if forgotten or misplaced, her blue eyes quizzical, anxious, putting out her velvet palm to stop passersby, asking passersby, other people's relatives, other people's friends and children, other old people in other wheelchairs crazier than herself *Where is the garden? Have they pulled it up? What about the peonies? They could do with a drink*, and it was a place her grandmother would not, not in any possible reality, return from.

Bea's hand had gone nerveless. Liam pulled their grandmother's nightdress down. The attendants rolled a sheet under her and lifted her swiftly onto their stretcher. The green blanket folded over her and sealed itself neatly like the flap of an envelope. Two straps followed, buckles clacking as they slid home. The grandmother's face had not altered. Her eyes did not open. Bea watched the attendants carry her downstairs and her grandmother was already gone from her. She stood under the roused cave of night the crickets' hymns echoing in an absence, Freddy sobbing by the window, Liam gently, clumsily, packing a small pink case with their grandmother's things. Underclothes, two nightgowns, socks, toothbrush. Her ice-blue clear plastic brush with bristles soft enough for a baby. Her favourite talcum powder. An hour before, Bea and Freddy had sponged and dried and sprinkled her with this powder and kissed in its encircling smell of lily-of-the-valley while their grandmother folded her skinny forefingers carefully into the hem of her towel and beamed softly, patiently, anticipating bed.

Liam snicked the catch on the pink case. He followed the attendants down the stairs. The night drew back. Bea listened to Freddy's sobs grow fainter. Probably he sobbed for more than their grandmother, he was sobbing for them too, for he and she, always withheld, always living forward into a hope that had failed to arrive, always parted as if by something like age or madness.

Freddy said: "Did you know I tried to cut my wrists too?"

Bea sat down where she was very carefully.

Eventually his crying stopped.

"We have to phone your parents," said Freddy. "Then we have to go with her."

"Sh," said Bea, getting up.

She took his hand and led him to their grandmother's bed. They climbed in under the fish-demons, into the small crumpled print of her body. The covers were still warm.

"I can feel her," Freddy said and began to cry again. Bea had imagined this moment, imagined he and she in this bed: she had seen herself lying stiff and excited and terrified and waiting, her heart ticking like a clock, while his hands moved heavily up her arms and lifted the dark cloth from her neck and carefully as if

93

it were her skin "I can't think of anything better to take off you," he would whisper, "than Grampa's old pyjamas," but he didn't. They turned into each other's arms and pressed together and held tightly while the bed spun, adrift, and held them in dark seas, and wept.

In the morning they woke to find the sun broken in a thousand rainbows by the crystals on their grandmother's lampshade. Freddy rolled onto Bea swiftly and his tongue lit a thousand channels through her limbs. He lifted his head. Some insurmountable thing showed in his algae-coloured eyes. Stricken by a movement larger than herself Bea put him aside and rose. She unbuttoned their grandfather's pyjama top and let it slide away. The pants followed. From where she stood in the dolloped light she saw him begin to shake.

She knelt under the looming headboard and laid her fingers over his mouth. He bit them gently. The movement crested, she recognized their old green wave finally descended, she found his chest under her hands and mouth and nipples, and opened, and sank.

Time stopped when the cicada sang. Bea's hand on the sheer curtain; the green light that came through the ivy dappling her wrist and the scar there. She could hear Frederick's voice down in the yard, husky from cigarettes and whiskey. Frederick's voice paused too, hung on the summer air like a wing. The cicada broke and the wing stooped, a soft soft glide into the grass.

Frederick was talking to Bea's mother. Bea was perched on the toilet-lid in the big upstairs bathroom at the farm. She still went there sometimes. The dappling green sunlight, the faintly wafting curtains, the tiled silence, settled her. Coincidentally it was also a place from which you could hear everything happening down on the drive, by the side gardens, or in the yard. Now Frederick was talking to Mrs. Chambers. Bea didn't try to make out the words, but she noticed her mother's tone of controlled grief, disapproval. In a different way she noticed Freddy's tone,

which never varied. He could say anything, be crude or impeccably polite, and Bea would understand the words second, if at all.
To Bea if not to him his voice was always: soft, dark, a torrent;
the beginning of a Niagara of the senses.

"...about Bea?" her mother was saying.

There was a pause. "She's all right," said Frederick. He kissed
his aunt, turned away, and got into his car. The car backed away
from the fence, swung round. Gravel on the drive rolled from
its wheels. The sound of the engine had faded when the cicada
began again.

Bea's mother tilted her head up. Tears made her eyes luminous. Her gaze found Bea at the window and held. He had said
to Bea: "If I go out west and I'm good, they'll give me my job
back." Said "I'm still lost, Bea" and touched her face.

"I know," her mother said suddenly. "I know." Her voice, soft
and thin, came up clearly to Bea from the garden.

Bea let the curtain drop.

She went down to her mother. "It's not so lonely without her,"
her mother said, taking Bea's hand. Bea nodded. They stood
listening. The cicada sang for them.

Truths and Epiphanies

Part One: The Season of Ordinary Time

Bea was twenty-eight years old and she had decided to cut the apron-strings at last. She'd decided. She was firm on it.

Everybody does it or has it done, she thought. It's common as dirt.

Predictably it was over a man. His name was Rupert. Since by now Bea told her mother everything, she told Claudine about Rupert. She told her she'd decided to ask him out and that they'd been giving it a try. She told her how, because they'd been friends for so long, the thing they had going was like a Victorian courtship. It was totally staid, it wasn't even twentieth-century, said Bea. It was like something arranged.

Bea was hoping to convey to her mother the difficulties of changing a friendship into love. It was a situation fraught with delicacies; she wanted her mother to understand and offer sympathy.

That it might actually be none of her mother's business did occur to Bea, but only vaguely. Once Bea had decided to divulge something she did so, finding the sense of accomplishment afterwards worth what she had suffered in self-exposure.

"Oh, no," Mrs. Chambers said. "Oh Beatrix. No."

Mrs. Chambers had a habit of thinking out loud and then feeling remorseful. Though on several occasions this had caused Bea pain she had come to appreciate it: Bea could depend on knowing Claudine's gut reaction to something before it had been

processed through her mother's formidable brain. In this case
Bea had known in advance what her mother would feel. Her
mother didn't approve of Rupert. Neither she nor Dr. Chambers
ever really had approved of Rupert. They found him low-class.
This was a verdict Bea considered absurd, given that if her own
family were to occupy a class it would have to have been wholly
invented for them. On the other hand she knew what Claudine
meant: unlike them, Rupert hadn't been to university. University
tended to leave language, manners, pronunciations, modes of
humour, that never quite rubbed off again. Rupert lacking these
things, of course, was partly what Bea found attractive about him.

She told her mother, knowing it would make everything
slightly easier on her, "We aren't sleeping together yet, if it makes
any difference."

It was a sop. Her mother had a tendency to think of Bea's
sex-life as if it were hers to dispense. Bea's father was even worse
on this score: something Bea had been able to identify, find
strangely touching, and ignore, for years.

More or less on cue her mother said: "Have you any idea how
much your father loves you?"

"I know," said Bea reasonably, though she didn't feel reason-
able. "I know he loves me. I love him. Only sometimes he loves
me like an extension of himself."

Her mother was silent. What her mother's silence meant was:
she was acknowledging a truth. Bea was right.

"For once in my life," Bea went on– Bea's conviction could
be slightly alarming whenever, as now, she was delivering verdicts
long since made in private– "I want from you the kind of love
that says: 'You know what you need to do.' You're trying to
protect me. You don't love me that way."

Accusatory as these statements were, they were speaking
normally. They were discussing. They never argued. Not any
more. Not since Bea was a teenager and her mother had hated
her clothes. Bea would always feel doomed, after Claudine
Chambers had denounced her clothes: it was Bea's particular
cast of mind to turn conflicts of taste into simple facts, in this

97

case: that she, Bea, was ugly. Bea however was also stubborn. In her mind the clothes and herself, ugly as they apparently were, *were* her. She couldn't change her*self*. That would be *lying*.

Claudine said now, in one of her flashes of insight, "No, you're right. We're not loving you like that."

"That's the kind of love I want," Bea said clearly.

Bea's father came in for lunch, and suspended their conversation. Dr. Chambers needed and ate meals as regularly as clock-work. This was unlike either of them and so became something they laughed about, grabbing muffins in mid-morning or chocolate and tea in mid-afternoon, buttering bread with peanut butter at 4 p.m. and making popcorn to watch movies on the VCR. (Her father could never stay awake for movies.) Her father went to the pantry now and poured himself a glass of wine standing by the pantry sink. He also decanted a half-litre for future use and taking his wine glass and decanter, went out, silent but directed, to sit on the porch. It was early summer, the sun bright and hot. Wind tossed the trees and goldfinches chattered around the eaves of the farmhouse. Her father's routine never varied. All his worn work-pants sagged in the bum; he would stand displaying them at the sink, pouring out his wine like a careful and slightly clumsy alchemist; he would take himself out to the summer-porch. It was his favourite place. There he would sit and drink, staring mutely at his kingdom, in the only brief respite he ever took from his labours of maintaining it.

Watching Henry Chambers leave the kitchen it occurred to Bea that perhaps her mother had compassion for the same solid, inarticulate activities in her father which she had compassion for in Rupert. But she didn't say it.

"I just want the best for you," her mother murmured.

She was cutting celery for Henry's salad plate. Bea stood on the other side of the counter away from her.

"I know Mum," said Bea. "I know that." She circled the counter and put her arms around her mother. Spontaneously then and without motive she told her mother she was her friend, she was her best friend. Bea had such respect for what she was and what she'd taught her; did she know how she was at the centre of everything she did or was that she cared about?

That was the trouble with them, Bea thought later. They made these elegant speeches. The complication was, they really meant them.

A couple of times in the sixties and seventies Bea's mother had made them matching aprons. Pinafore style was in vogue; they were long, full, bibbed aprons with high ruffles over the shoulders and lace in two lines down the bodice. Bea and her mother would put them on and move like queens through the kitchen, royalty come to slum for a day. Both of them were negligent cooks. Bea would begin to bake and Claudine would put in a roast she would later forget about and then Claudine would retreat with mock screams from Bea's mess. Hearing her mother's mock screams Bea would make the mess worse, throw eggs exuberantly into bowls, toss flour in and out of bins and cups, knead and mix everything with her hands, littering the counter with ingredients. Bea had found one of the aprons recently. It hadn't been worn for a long time. She'd kept it wrapped carefully in plastic. She unwrapped it, tried it on, and sent it off to the Good Will. She had shrunk since then. It was too big to be useful. The voluptuous country teenager– Bea would say "fat" and Claudine would say, offended, "you were *never fat*"– had been urbanized. Claudine now sometimes called Bea "an-orexic." Bea would always rise to the bait, get angry with her because while anorexics had no bums, the bum Bea didn't have was her mother's, and her mother had never had one either. They'd make their ritualistic, brief, heated exchange on the subject of Bea's weight. Then they would drag Bea's father into the car after dinner and go out for ice cream cones in town.

Bea was, in fact, the same size as Claudine's own mother, who had been smaller than Claudine. Thus it was possible, Bea supposed, that in her own way she might also be as stubborn. "Irene Sigurdsen," Bea's uncles would say, her cousins Nicholas and Frederick. "*No-one* was more stubborn than Irene." Mrs.

Chambers added:

"*Mother would argue black was white to protect someone she loved.*"

But then, *my* mother is like that, thought Bea.

Claudine had made the aprons because she loved to sew. At age six Claudine sat beside her mother while Irene worked at a treadle machine and sewed tiny dolls' clothes by hand for her collection of forty dolls. Claudine told Bea how offended she'd been when, at age eight, her Brownie leader had thought her mother helped her sew those doll-clothes. She told Bea about the Brownie leader with a lingering echo of offended dignity. They would fish for a picture in the photograph albums. Bea's mother at age seven, her crooked grin copied from a favourite teacher, the black gap between her front teeth. Claudine's uncles had teased her unmercifully about the gap between her teeth and later after she'd married Bea's father she'd had it fixed.

In the picture, Claudine at seven sat slouched in a party-dress on the lawn beside her parents' lily-garden, surrounded by the "favourites" of her forty dolls. With Irene's help she had held an elaborate tea-party for them. Irene had suggested– she'd never insisted with Claudine, she didn't have to– that Claudine choose only her favourite dolls to invite. Claudine had agreed. But she was tender-hearted. She sat with thirty-three dolls tipped together, posed stiffly in hand-edged bonnets and their best dresses. The dolls stared boldly out with the confidence of those adored. Bea's mother as a child grinned crookedly at the camera from her pride-of-place, supreme mama at age seven. Claudine and Bea would look at this picture and Bea would say, as she or her brothers had often said: "Mum, we owe our existence to your dolls," firmly believing it, especially for those near the bottom of the family: through her dolls, they believed, Claudine had become accustomed to a landscape of babies.

She had graduated from sewing doll-clothes to sewing clothes for her family. Claudine would tell Bea that she'd thought herself highly mature when she'd set out into married life, at age twenty, with Bea's father. She'd borne Bea's oldest brothers in quick succession: Arthur when she was twenty-one, Donald at twenty-two, Rainer at twenty-three. Francis at twenty-five. Duncan at twenty-seven and then nothing; a lull. Bea would wonder about this. Weren't they trying hard, did something force them to wait, didn't it go well, was her mother taking a rest before Bea? She had made her mother wait. Almost three years. She'd had no girls. *Poor Mrs. Chambers,* said the nurses as Claudine came into Devonshire General and delivered another boy. The nurses knew Dr. Chambers and were fond of his jokes, and felt sorry for him. *No girls.*

The day Bea was born the shift had just changed, but the nurses didn't go home. Her mother described them to Bea, faces filling the pane of the operating-room door, eyes wide, mouths ajar, craning to see if the Chambers would be in luck. Bea came out. Claudine brought her forth. Bea's mother told Bea that the doctor had immediately put her on Claudine's belly, and then couldn't pry them apart to wash her.

Her mother clutched Bea tightly and was wheeled back to her room.

"You cannot know what it is," she would say to Bea, "to get a baby the same sex as yourself. I loved every baby and I never wanted my boys to be girls. But when you came it was different... I couldn't believe you were real."

She finally let them take Bea to the nursery, where the nurses coddled her as if she had been their own. There weren't many other babies in the nursery in November: the other three, two girls and a boy, became friends of Bea's in high school. Bea would be brought to her mother at feeding times with a kiss-curl on her forehead and a pink bow in her weedy hair.

Less than an hour after the birth the gifts and flowers had started arriving. Bea still had the gold-filled bracelet which had been sent to her from an aunt in Toronto; it had her name, spelled wrong, and the date. She also had the silver baby cup, tarnished, her name spelled wrong on that too. Claudine's hospital room was buried in flowers. The way Claudine told it

Bea was forced to see their small town as if ignited at 8:00 am. by rumours of her birth. A lot of people knew Claudine and Henry Chambers. Things kept arriving. The doll with dark curly hair and one eyelid that winked arrived before the stores were open. Bea's mother recalled and noted such details: to what length gift-givers had gone, because Bea was born before business hours. A bank of gladioli came. The stems were four feet long and they'd had to stand on the floor. A nurse had carried them to Claudine's bedside. "Where should I put these flowers, Mrs. Chambers?" she'd asked. Bea's mother had looked at the card, which was signed "The Milkman." "Oh," said Claudine airily, "just stand them in the corner, they're from the milkman." The nurse blushed and fled, convinced, said Claudine to Bea, that the new Chambers baby was the product of an affair.

"But of course," Claudine would explain, "I'd recognized your father's hand-writing."

Henry Chambers had been present at his wife's delivery. He'd gone out afterwards, to shave and change; though he never delivered his own babies he'd attended all their births long before this was fashionable, and before it was even respectable. Claudine stayed in hospital for a week. "Basking," she said, in all the attention. Bea basked in the nursery under the ministrations of several nurses. Though the dice were loaded against her, Claudine had rolled doubles. They had rolled them: Bea and her mother; her father.

Inevitably Bea would see herself as Claudine described her birth. She saw a baby self, helpless and agreeable, a sponge for both the commotion and the coddling. She would think of the commotion, the coddling, and grow ambivalent, glad to have been wanted and to hear how much, ashamed or apologetic about all the attention. She would wonder what her friends' mothers had thought, her brothers who'd heard the story, maybe too many times, Jeffrey and Liam who'd come after her and had not been more girls; she would wonder if her brothers felt neglected or second-rate, if they resented her, and if all the attention had spoiled them somehow, spoiled she and her mother, so that they hungered for a steady diet of such attention now. She would wonder if this celebration at her birth, which she owed to her five preceding brothers, and about which she could do nothing, had set for her mother some fatal and erroneous standard of Bea's worth, a standard that was parting them now.

Claudine made them matching pant-suits and shorts sets. One was moss-green plaid. They knew now that they both looked ghastly in moss-green, but in those days they had worn whatever colours were featured in the magazines; Bea remembered the outfits, jackets with brass buttons, Bermuda shorts, the flannel exquisitely thin, like a second skin, dry and soft over her own. It never occurred to Bea that she would not want to look like her mother. When she got to be a teenager and suddenly wore what she did it wasn't out of perversity, as Mrs. Chambers had firmly believed, nor to spite her parents or the family; she had just changed. That was all.

Claudine had also put Bea into miniskirts. This was long before anyone in their rural farming community would have been caught dead in one and the skirts were killingly short: for some of them she had made Bea matching panties. Fortunately Bea had Claudine's legs, which were actually Irene's legs; in her miniskirts, at first anyway, Bea had felt proud, free, privileged.

Claudine, however, could not walk the halls of Bea's small country public school. She was blind to how strange Bea might actually seem there. She would whisper to Bea at school concerts, looking at the starched white blouses and the wool kilts that fell below the knees of the other children, "They don't look like little girls in long skirts like that." What Bea heard her say, though she never said it, was: "Feel sorry for those poor girls. Their mothers don't know any better." Bea would look at them, and when they were being teased at recess, she would feel pity: not because they were being teased but because they had such mothers, who weren't abreast of everything Out There, whose imaginations did not rove beyond school or county. Farm boys chased a soccer ball across the school yard. They were skinny and their white skulls flashed through their brush-cuts in the autumn sun. Bea's brothers read in corners of the field or presided with the ponderous judiciousness of intellectuals over noon-hour baseball games, their hair thick and past their ears, brushing the collars of their Nehru jackets. Claudine and her sewing lady (by then she had always needed help) had made the jackets for them carefully at home after a trip to Florida with Bea's father. In Florida Claudine had seen all the young men wearing them. Bea, in school, would think of her mother sewing in quiet afternoons, the farm-house empty and flooded just past the window-frames by sun, the centres of rooms comfortable and gloomy. She would look out her classroom window across the concession to their barn lifting its roof out of the trees. She would think with longing of her mother at home alone doing the things she did, quietly, walls around her protecting her and the whole of the farm outside. While her mother sat in the house across three fields and four bands of trees and just beyond their barn Bea's loneliness had a taste, like the smell of leaf-smoke or green walnut skins. She would think of the farm. Below their barn the pond and honeysuckles and woods would be still, gilded in sunshine, waiting for her brothers and her to get off the school bus and go down to play there. After school her mother would let them make snacks and then she would send them out, banished from TV shows they thought they couldn't live without; they'd walk back swinging sticks and eating pears from the ground to float woolly-bear caterpillars across the leaden, cold pond on leaves.

Bea had not been a bad student. She had missed nothing she was required by adults not to miss.

Instead, missing her mother, she missed whatever it might have been to belong with other girls. Girls around Bea shouted, giggled, squealed, simpered at boys, anchored themselves in each other's tenuous friendship; they stripped for gym class chattering beside the sinks while Bea changed alone in a cubicle. Later, when Bea was desperate to join them, it was already too late. She didn't know how. She was unprepared for the loss of dignity which changing her mind entailed; it did not occur to her that one might survive such contradictions. The other girls flashed their training-bras at nine and ten while Claudine took Bea downtown to buy her undershirts. Bea felt trapped, caught between her mother's innocence and her own. Claudine was the mother, she was supposed to know that Bea was too old for undershirts; Bea was the child, supposed to benefit from her mother's perfect awareness and concern. Bea knew these things. Imbued however with Claudine's own respect for social institutions such as parenthood, she said nothing. At age 14 she waited silently for her turn at the 50-yard dash and when it came, pressed her elbows to her breasts again so they wouldn't bounce, and ran. She hid her embarrassment in cubicles. She looked out the high transom windows of the washroom and thought of her mother and hid her, protecting her from small girls who, if she had gone out there now, would have known that her mother had failed somehow. At home, Bea protected her mother as much as she could from her difference by saying nothing.

She would go out to her pony. Once mounted everything would mysteriously slip away. She didn't care if her breasts bounced. She rode to meet her one friend, Charlene, who rode too. Their fathers had gotten them the ponies.

By sixteen Bea hadn't known how to protect her mother any more. Though she still cared, she could no longer afford to.

There would be fights. Her mother and father sat her down and, in the context of Francis's current relationship, of which they disapproved, her father said to her while her mother listened: "Always choose a partner from the head, not the heart."

Bea jumped up. She was full of outrage for her brother Francis and for her own devalued heart. She cried. She disagreed violently, pacing back and forth. Her father said to her: "Oh, stop acting like a clown." Believing this to be the final degradation, Bea ran out the front door.

Her mother came after her. She put her arm round Bea while Bea sobbed and tried to shake it off. Bea didn't now remember how she'd gotten back into the house. Later that weekend, still nursing her adolescent devastation, she'd said the word "Shit!" loudly over something and her mother had lectured her for an hour, with the personal woundedness only Claudine Chambers could muster, on her appalling insensitivity to have used that word at home. Claudine began to cry. Bea opened and closed drawers in the living room: polished old wood drawers that opened and closed smoothly, fashioned by Irish or English or Scottish craftsmen. The furniture had been handed down to them from any one of several branches of deceased and shadowy relatives; Bea played with the drawers while her mother talked, her voice breaking. Bea was sullen and silent. From time to time she affected an intellectual line of defense, talking down to her mother as if she didn't know anything about the real world.

Five or six years later her mother had spilled her purse by accident. She had said unthinkingly, "Oh *shit*," and then looked at Bea and they had both started laughing.

But, in fact, it had been true that they knew nothing about the real world. Now, at age 28, Bea was beginning to hear her parents admit it. "We had no idea," they would say, her father wonderingly and her mother matter-of-factly, "we really thought we were like everybody." This translated, Bea knew, as *We thought everybody was like us.* In spite of her mother's innocent beliefs Gordie Hurder at age 9 spewed a line of *fucks* and *shits* that would have left a longshoreman pale. Bea sat in the row beside him and after a whole lunch-hour of Gordie Hurder's largely vainglorious but she knew now, feisty, curses, she could feel her stomach roll, her face drain. At the same time, as one of her grade's half-dozen over-achievers she was called upon to be cynical and unimpressed by the word "fuck" uttered at 9, because to be impressed was to be no better than Gordie Hurder, who was flunking and whose father was a junkman.

In a rain of childish profanity Bea honed her persona. She made it as firm and unassailable as the girdles she would sometimes secretly haul from the back of her mother's dresser and try on. She had known Claudine never wore those girdles any more; nevertheless they convinced her that to grow up would be horrible. Persona shored her up and inside it her sensibilities and delicacies, which were in fact Claudine's, remained safe from public ridicule. Outside she was blasé; inside, where she and her mother were one, they were alone.

Such were Bea's days while Claudine sat at home sewing. At home with the untrammelled sun, the burnished trees, the bluejays taking seeds from the drooped heads of the sunflowers they'd planted in spring. She sat sewing Nehru collars she'd admired in Florida, beside the corner cabinet full of family photographs. A roast beef sent its dark thick smell through the downstairs of the house. She sewed while the mending languished in a box. Bea's father complained about missing shirts which had lost buttons; her brothers' jeans with the knees out grew crumpled and too small on the bottom of the box. Out of desperation all of them had learned to sew. Duncan intoned: "Old clothes never die, they just go to the sewing," and they laughed. They would repeat this saying now, their mother's habits a matter of family legend. They would recall the day Jeffrey put a sign on the fridge. Their father was always dragging greening and mouldy bits of leftover food from the back shelves of the refrigerator and pontificating about waste. Their mother would tell him regally: "You don't have to carry on about them, just throw them out," opening the funnel of the garbage disposal. To Bea she would whisper furiously, if Bea pulled out something spoiled, "Quick! Throw it out before your father sees!" She would press it into the bottom of the garbage-pail, throwing a few orange-peels or a cereal box over it. Bea's father had always hated waste. He hadn't known, Bea thought, that with style and originality came madness, a prodigality and waste as ineradicable as nature's. Jeffrey had taped on the fridge in script approximating runes:
NATIONAL ARCHIVES OF EGYPT AND MESOPOTAMIA.
Once he'd posted his Christmas list there in the form of a scroll. It unwound from wooden handles made of old molding

he'd tacked on in the basement and it implored the reader for a lot of hockey equipment and *Reader's Digests*. Many Christmases later Claudine still had it, in her cupboards and drawers with their baby pictures and Bea's first sketches, and illustrated sayings Bea would put up on the same fridge crediting other authors but if she'd made the sayings up, too shy to credit herself.

"Do you remember when you were a little kid," (wrote Bea, all of seventeen), "picking dandelions for her mother? They looked like little gold suns, and you got the stems too short, and by the time you gave them to her they had closed up. And she would smile, and put them in a cut-glass vase on the centre of the table as if they had been long-stemmed yellow roses.

"Because, of course, they were."

Bea put that on the fridge. Claudine kept it somewhere.

They'd referred to it from time to time over the years, no longer as something Bea illustrated and gave, nor as something Claudine inspired, but as a statement of principle, their philosophy of hope.

They could repeat it only when Bea came to visit. She didn't live at the farm any more and hadn't of course for a long time. Bea had moved on to the city to school and there were new things they'd shared, even if Claudine couldn't know it. Darker things, almost adult: flirtations with chemicals, delinquent company, days without sleep and entertainments best forgotten and vintage suit jackets Bea admired at parties that were then given her by men who wanted her favours. The men were drunk. Bea was not. She took the suit jackets happily and walked home alone at 2 a.m.

Sitting at home she would alter the suit jackets to fit her idea of style, bent over them in the gloom of her paint-daubed loft with a sewing needle.

Lunch was over. Bea's father discreetly left the table to pick his teeth. This was a habit Claudine abhorred and which Bea laughed at her for abhorring. Bea sided with him. She saw nothing tragic, as her mother did, in her father picking his teeth after meals. It was the only way she knew him. Presumably it was the only way her mother knew him too, but Claudine carried her ideal scenarios, her rewritten scripts. She would look at people; seeing how they were, she would make plans: create unlikely romances, plot surprise meetings, dream away their flaws, imagine their talents all developed: always, in her mind, re-ordering their lives according to her vision of what they needed to be happy. Sometimes she would try to enact her scenarios. Sometimes they worked, though never exactly as planned. A friend of hers who was a minister had named this habit once: he'd called it *manipulating for God*. Bea had been relieved then, and was comforted now, by the idea that there might be such a thing—especially since she had a sneaking suspicion she was prone to the same behaviour.

Bea and her mother looked at each other in the sun on the porch, over the ruins of their salad plates. They knew they would not resolve anything. Bea was hard still. She felt somehow misused. Her mother started to reach for her but she had risen. She banged the screen door as she went out.

She walked on the gravel roads all afternoon, litanizing as she went the familiar laneways and ditches. The trees, the bare field that used to hold a dilapidated barn, the junk dealer's at the corner where white geese rushed out hissing from rusty pickups in the yard. Everything was full of feeling. The white geese, the driveways, the gravel under her feet. She was angry at them. Though she had tried to exorcise them all through painting, they still held her; she had walked too many times on that road, passed the same trees and laneways too many times. They had grown indelible. They could not be erased by painting; they were printed. The mark of her mother's hand on her arm, which she had avoided by going out, banging the screen door, was warm on her skin anyway. Why do I need her approval? Bea asked herself this. She asked it and knew that she did not need her mother's approval. She wanted it. It was her weakness. She wanted those whose love had in the end been sure, if strange;

constant; and ultimately, she thought, had not harmed her, to flag her actions as good ones. Whomever she'd carried through the halls of her school, the long afternoon hours in the smell of eraser staring over fields at the roof of their barn, seemed to Bea after everything was tallied up a small enough price to pay.

I paid though, thought Bea. I did pay. Give me my due now. If you have to suffer for me, do it in silence.

It was her mother who taught Bea the liturgical seasons: Advent, Christmas, Epiphany, Lent, Easter, Pentecost, and the Season of Ordinary Time. The Chambers attended church every Sunday, as had both Claudine's and Henry's families; Claudine had been raised Anglican and Henry Methodist, but when the Methodists joined the United Church Henry's family had gone over, and Claudine had found it compatible enough: the Chambers had all gone to the United Church in Devonshire. Sunday morning after her father's porridge Bea and her brothers would be sent up to get into church clothes; the church clothes felt stiff and confining and so they would make it as far as the upstairs front hall before engaging in pillow fights or bumping down the stairs in blankets. After the service, on high holy days, Claudine wouldn't let any of them change until they'd posed for family pictures on the lawn. As a result the liturgical seasons also hovered in family photographs: Bea's father and brothers looking uncomfortable in grey flannel, Bea and her mother in homemade velvets, Easter a sere spring, Thanksgiving russets and purples, Christmas red interiors, the in-between times a steady pentecostal green. Meanwhile, inside the house, at every one of the old Christian festivals, there was celebration.

Valentine's Day Bea and her brothers would come home from school to the table laid with the red-and-white-checked cloth. Each placemat was a white lace paper doily. Her mother had used the good white water goblets and the pink and white English china; there would be cards for all of them in red or pink envelopes and dishes of red cinnamon hearts and white peppermints, a roast chicken with gold skin and apple cider frozen from fall, a white cake with pink icing Claudine had made and decorated herself. Red cardboard cupids with quivers, holding hearts, dangled from the lights or stood on tiptoe in a pot of red tulips in the centre of the table. The flowers were Claudine's, from Henry. They'd been accompanied by tall Valentine cards with jokes about long marriages; occasionally his valentine would be achingly sentimental and they took these rarer cards to be the truthful ones.

On the evening of Pancake Tuesday they ate pancakes, the meal enlivened by its not being breakfast. Bea's mother would drown hers in maple syrup. Her father would tell her she was being wasteful, and she would tell him to eat his supper and never mind hers. At their various places along the table, Bea and her brothers would make lakes of maple syrup overflow their spongy stacks. On St. Patrick's Day the cake was green. The plant in the centre given faithfully to Claudine by Henry would be a live shamrock sprouting yellow bloom. While Bea had gazed out the classroom window waiting for the final bell to ring, for the bus pulling up outside, her mother had been cutting four-leafed clovers out of green construction paper and putting them at all their places. A few dangled on green threads where the cupids and their quivers had hung.

Christmas was a riot of gifts. They overflowed the feet of the tree and spread a tide of beribboned papery shapes into the room. Bea's mother and father loved to put the tree up early; at the family's height they'd had three Christmas trees, one for each of the playrooms and the living room. The trees stood in bay windows, to be seen at night above the coloured lights on the bushes. The pass-through between kitchen and playroom dripped with cotton batting snow; on the table under the kitchen clock and in the living room there were manger scenes. Bea was always delegated to set them up. She would arrange plastic animals and plastic kings and shepherds in tableaux, dramas half-enacted, each figure positioned obliquely or directly towards the manger depending on whether they had been there for some time or had just arrived, and depending what they thought of their own worthiness to be there at all. She would correct their placements after rearrangement by other children. Mary and the animals always dreamed close to the plastic Child, whose fists waved stiffly above the plastic straw. Under them Bea had put real straw brought from the barn. It was too slippery. Once or twice instead she'd used dead brown fern gathered in the woods, before settling on hay. From then on the kings laboured in long robes through foot-tangling alfalfa towards an already closed, contented Mother bending over her half-buried Child.

Each Sunday in Advent they lit another candle in the Advent wreath. The season advanced and the flames grew in numbers as the candles shrank, flooding wax over pine boughs and red berries Claudine had clipped from bushes round the cold yard and arranged at the wreath's base. On Christmas Eve they lit the single white central Christ-candle; the five candles would blaze out over a table buried under food. Turkey and cranberry sauce (Claudine always made the sauce herself), squash, mashed potatoes, peas, beans, three kinds of salad, red and white wine; mince and apple pies, shortbread, gingerbread, coconut stacks, chocolate squares, sugar cookies shaped liked stars and Santas, chocolates, peppermint patties, ice water in the extra glasses. The white linen cloth was laid with the good silver, the crystal goblets, the cranberry glasses and Claudine's mother's flowered china. Claudine sat at the end nearest the kitchen in her best dress and jewellery. Bea's father sat at the opposite end, in horn rimmed glasses and black velvet jacket, knife poised over the breast of the roast. Bea's grandfather would say grace, or her father; after their grandfather had died it became her mother who always said grace. Henry preferred hers.

Once Bea was old enough she loved to do the centrepieces herself. Her mother liked her to do them, and they become co-conspirators, Bea her mother's apprentice. "It has your special artistic touch," Claudine would say to Bea. When everyone had sat down her father would lead the exclamations. Bea sometimes wondered now how it was that eventually she felt diminished by her adherence to the family's beautifying rituals. She thought it was in the picture of herself their praise gave back to her: someone flickering and not-quite-substantial, someone who touched down and dusted something transparent into an arrangement of objects, the rest of the time invisible. She would sit at the table hearing the appreciation, feeling already gone.

And yet, Bea thought calmly, I'm really just perverse. She was suspicious of compliments, in general, and that was uncharitable and skewed. Her mother had lived with the same problem all the years she had provided for them. It was only what every mother knows: she who makes things beautiful for others is a slave to the beauty. Whatever she creates becomes inaccessible to her, a construct carrying too much of herself and so, less power to move her; until Bea or her mother would turn in a moment, as Bea always did, at Christmas by the lit tree in early morning, at Easter over the pass-through loaded with the lilies Henry had given her their long white trumpets fragrant in the dark, and she would be there: inside the festival itself. She would feel dragged by the long train of history, the tide of the archetypal celebrations closed over her head, and something unnamable was all around. Her mother had summoned the unnamable thing. She had made the shrines, napkins and paper cupids, and the rest arrived.

Bea's cynical brother Francis turned fourteen and began to make black-humoured remarks about the excess. He muttered obscenities to the plastic dwarfs and protested sourly when the string of the bell that played "Jingle Bells" was pulled. By sixteen Bea was beginning to repeat his remarks to herself, laughing over his misanthropic witticisms when her mother couldn't hear and be hurt. As the family aged, they grew out of the excess. The excess was also, Bea realized, her mother's innocence. It was Claudine's fearlessness, her determination that things would be only as she saw them.

A determination, Bea thought, which had extended also and still did extend, to her children.

When Bea came back it was dinner-time. Her mother's eyes looked stained. Bea's chest felt like a bell that had been struck:

one deep but clamorous note hummed there without diminishing.

In the evening, Claudine proposed to Dr. Chambers that, since Bea was home, they should drive to the gardens of his friend who bred irises. It was the height of iris season. Her father's face lit up. He looked at Bea grinning, his arm reaching for her shoulders, and pulled her to him. Her chair, beside him at the dinner table, rocked slightly. Her mother did this: invented peace offerings. She couldn't stand discord, her elastic mind would spring to a distraction; all Bea's life her mother's talent with children had been inexhaustible because of this skill. She could distract them from whining, from bad behaviour, something they shouldn't touch or shouldn't eat, in such a way that they were happy to be distracted. Bea looked at her mother. Their glance acknowledged the offering. She took her father's hand. The enormity of his affection, its innocence, its freedom from inventiveness and any attendant darkness, his simplicity, which was her father's talent, were the things that could always, eventually, humble them both.

The three of them drove to the iris farm. When they got out of the car they were in a weedy field that squeaked with crickets under early evening sun. They walked along a path. Bea's father, garrulous as always, went to greet his friends. She and her mother wandered slightly distant along a worn footpath beside a high cedar hedge. When they came round it Bea forgot the issue of Rupert for a moment: spreading out before them, banked against wind by huge hedges of blooming spirea, marched row after row of curled and feathery iris heads. Long meandering rainbow-coloured drifts, the sun beginning to set; bare earth, gold straw laid between the rows, and over them the sky burnt orange. The air was indescribable with smells. She and her mother walked forward at the same time. They were mute. They wandered up and down the rows; Bea looked at her mother and her mother was one row over and down, waist high in a pool of petals as big as her hands. The two of them leaned, cupped, sniffed. Bea's row ended. When she looked for her mother again she had disappeared.

She gazed round the empty field of flowers. She imagined being her mother, wandering through the rows, thinking about Bea; she observed where she would go. She turned a corner in the hedge. Her mother was there. Claudine had stopped in a sudden pocket of lilac scent. Her way was blocked by lilac and she stood, her pale figure etched against the dark foliage by falling dusk. Just above her tipped-up head, mauve lilac bloom smudged the dusk like smoke. "Oh, Beatrix, smell," her mother was saying. They stood, eyes closed under the purple heap of the bush, breathing in. Her mother said: "I could be in heaven." Something about how she said it, something about the state Bea was in, following an image from field to hedge, around a corner: something made Bea recognize everything about this place, everything in it seemed constant because of her mother.

The note that wouldn't stop ringing cracked and fell into silence. Evening birds chirped close in the hedge. Bea saw the inevitability of her mother's death as if it had happened. It was spring. It was the high season for lilacs. Her mother was gone. Bea was there without her, remembering Claudine under the mauve smoke of this bush, heaping its fragrant branches on her grave to make this moment return. From a different side of the grave she was yet reaching to extort her mother's love. Bea leaned forward with her mother now to smell. Her hand found her mother's shoulder for balance. In the scented air she sucked in was their connection and something else, mortality, the temerity of any earthly heaven caught in a smell or a person.

She felt expanded or small. She thought then that her mother was beautiful, caring, assured, graceful, extraordinary. She thought: you are unlike anybody. She thought she was these things not only because she was her mother but because, Bea suddenly suspected, she was also the daughter of two who, if they could have been brought there tonight, if they had been still alive, would have stood just so, outlined against the leaves, and breathed. Bea thought of her grandmother Irene, whose heart could turn black to white.

Later they said goodnight. Bea's mother hugged her. Bea understood her mother as someone she would not have forever. There was the scent of lilacs in her hair. On her hands round Bea's shoulders were the root beer, orange, and chocolate smells of the blooms. They didn't let go for a while. Her mother was in the middle of a speech. She was saying to Bea: "The vision of that field is still in front of my eyes," meaning it, like all their speeches, her face bewildered. Bea let her go. Her mother said, "Have a good sleep, honey. Dream about the irises."

On her own fingers as Bea pulled the pillow round later were the smells of flower and steering wheel. She was back in the city; she'd borrowed Rupert's car and he'd needed it back. Even mortality couldn't undermine stubbornness.

Bea had taken on Rupert; it was about sex, but also more. She enjoyed her summer. She and Rupert played pool; they drank. Evenings she forgot the smell of the field in the smells of sweat and smoke. They drove down to the farm on weekends. Her father would be silent and avoid Rupert around the house; embarrassed, Rupert would go out to fish for long hours. Bea knew what was going on but refused to acknowledge it. Nor did she talk to Rupert. Black was white. Her mother loved her and would change her mind. This, in turn, would change her father. Claudine herself would sometimes glance at Bea with secret stern messages when they arrived on the side stoop; but Bea was ignoring her. The summer passed. Rupert threw the fish back. He and Bea returned to the streets and pool halls, to his bed where Bea went now proud to forget. Victorian courtship had given way; intimacies of friendship which could survive proximity had travelled.

Rupert had a thinnish body, pale because of auburn hair. His hair was thick and wavy. His skin glowed. Not translucently like her mother's nor darkly like her father's and brothers', but with a kind of ruddy light. She would spend spare hours recalling this light. Autumn came on. She found a new studio. Art interested her intermittently. They did not visit the farm. Rupert took Bea to see his brother and while Rupert's brother was making Bea laugh, rolling joints the size of his index finger in a basement bar, she realized she had not seen her own brothers for a long time.

When Bea phoned Jeffrey, he told her, angry and agitated, that she mustn't visit their parents any more unless she was alone. The summer had been too much for them, he said, especially their mother. Bea ought to have more consideration. Furthermore he, Jeffrey, did not like Rupert either, not for Bea and not in general.

It was, Bea thought anyway, long past lilac time. Autumn made death obvious, and banal. She was fierce Irene her grandmother; only the object of loyalty changed. She and her mother had parted company over a man. Bea phoned Mrs. Chambers and told her she wouldn't be joining the family for Thanksgiving.

It hurt, much more than Bea had expected.

Bea's mother had confessed relief when Bea told her she wouldn't bring Rupert there any more.

"Your father– " she said.

"It's your house," Bea said. "You have the right to be comfortable in it."

Then she'd added that she wouldn't be home for Thanksgiving. She heard her own wounds go down through her mother's voice: the confusion, the bewilderment. When Bea got off the phone she was shocked at her callousness. She addressed her mother silently. How could you be so confused? How dare you be so innocent?

Hypocrisy, Bea had thought, was a thing they'd both come to loathe. She thought: How dare you fail to understand. She thought: Giving thanks is a thing you taught me how to do.

At Thanksgiving for more than half Bea's life it had been her who set the table. She would spend the afternoon at it; female relatives and sisters-in-law, guests, would tiptoe around Bea's brooding study of her work, immanent in their respectful footfalls that picture which flitted briefly through Bea's concentration: the artist as they saw her, someone like a Black Hole, to whom space must be left for wilful moods, inexplicable pondering. Bea would arrange wild grapes and walnuts and butternuts. Cobs of corn with the dry husks pulled back, chestnuts and Indian corn, gourds, thorn haws, basswood nuts, coloured leaves and a small pumpkin her mother would have bought at the Devonshire market for her on Saturday; wild apples gathered under trees in the woods, dry weeds and grasses, the purple wild asters her mother called "Michaelmas daisies," picking armfuls when they went back through the fields on autumn walks. A vase of chrysanthemums from the garden, still breathing cold fall air. She would also press into service every silver candlestick ever given to her mother by adoring elderly relatives who'd pitied Claudine her giant brood. It all spilled from the gold cornucopia basket she kept in a high cupboard and took down for Bea every year.

The morning after Thanksgiving dinner Bea would creep down to look at her creation. The leaves' colour would be draining and their edges curled up, the berries had wrinkled, spilled wax and crumbs from her mother's pies decorated the tablecloth. She would sit in the dark early morning dining room. In a sort of bittersweet aftermath she would recall each detail of turkey, stuffing, sauce, gravy and salads, squares, cheese, wine, pies. Bea would see them ranged round the periphery of the great oak dining-table. The table itself had a myth attached to it. It had come over on a ship with Admiral Fitzsimmons, founder of Devonshire, and ended up somehow at the Chambers' church, used for banquets for years, until the Women's Auxiliary re-placed it with pressboard stacking tables. Henry, mind always on waste, had gone to the Women's Auxiliary. What were they going to do with the table? It was so old, they told him, they were going to throw it out. Henry gave them a donation and with the help of Donald, Arthur, Rainer, Francis, and a borrowed half-ton truck, delivered Admiral Fitzsimmons' table to a friend who did refinishing. Two months later they brought the table home. It was five feet wide, and had turned pillar legs, as big around as Bea's thigh, spaced at intervals along its length. At its shortest it was ten feet but a handle inserted in one end unwound the table along a central spindle to a length of 40. The most Bea had seen seated at it was 26; gatherings that hovered around 20 were more common. She sat at the corner of Admiral Fitzsimmons' table, near one end. She looked out over its expanse, at her centrepiece now showing its weaknesses and flaws. She saw them all there, the Chambers, in their places along each side. They were reaching and passing, laughing, commenting on each other's wine consumption, repeating absurdly exaggerated stories; re-playing comedy for their father, whose hearing was bad, playing jokes on Liam who liked to hoard his food, on Jeffrey who liked to steal other peoples'. They jollied grandchildren sulking over mounds of cold squash. They reported who had not closed their eyes during Blessing. Two sisters-in-law had a heart-to-heart. They ate, drank, talked, round endlessly flowing emptied plates or glasses needing refills. The dining room would grow warm; the noise level would mount and subside, in irregular bursts, to the chink of cutlery on china. The candles would burn down. Those who were romantic, which meant Bea, her mother, the grand-children, Duncan, Donald, and Rainer, would defend the can-dles against those who were practical and wished to blow them out, which meant Henry, Liam, or Jeffrey's wife Diane. A grandchild would relight one that had gone out on its own. Claudine would delegate victims to clear the table, and begin serving the next course with the calm of an experienced general.

Bea had never painted the feasts, which was what they were. She had only, so far, dared the empty table. Not the table exactly: Bea did not do realism. Her painting was recognizable, but there was something else: the lenthening of shadow, of colour, the slanting or diffusing of light. She sat in the morning summoned not by images but by the feeling which attended them: it was at Admiral Fitzsimmons' table that the family bonded and grew powerful, joining and flipping their secret wounds and losses.

Claudine had taught her how to give thanks. Never hypocrit-ically; letting gratitude be pure; allowing for enthusiasm.

Rupert drove trains. He grew up in a suburb in a small brick house. He came back from work smelling of cold outdoor air and diesel-fuel, they smoked a cigarette or two, he had auburn hair, his voice was like car tires swishing over their gravel roads.

Part Two: Advent

Claudine lived by hope, but her policy was inventiveness. Bea thought it was partly her remedy for being absent-minded. Some would say she was absent-minded because she was trying to do so much, blithely making herself answerable to so many people: her peers buckled at the work entailed by families of four but on top of her ten Bea's mother was always volunteering in town. Bea began to suspect that the absences, the burned dinners her father joked about, the Christmases where her mother could be counted on to have a fall or burst into tears, children forgotten for an hour at swimming practice, cookies so well hidden from teenage appetites that they couldn't be found, were evidence of a separate thing: her mother's eccentricity, evidence of her genius. Bea thought about the cliché of the absent-minded professor. She had lived her mother's re-invention of it: the absent-minded mother. Motherhood as much some eccentric gift as any professor's talent in a classroom.

The classroom defined them. Who was pupil, who student, had shifted constantly in Bea's childhood and still shifted; who stood at the front of the room and who, understanding their need to stand there, allowed them the privilege. Bea thought, when she instructed her mother in her feelings and her version of her mother's disregard for them, that she was in control, that she was instructing her mother about her life. Now it occurred to Bea that her mother was as familiar with Bea, a certain Bea, as Bea was, more familiar: that in her mother's listening, her agreeing, one might detect tolerance.

Bea failed to resent this. Claudine had offered Bea inventive-ness as if it were proof, the only proof, of a life well-lived. Bea had had to do a grade five project on weeds. Claudine took her for a walk after school to the ditches and the edges of the autumn fields where they collected teazle, ragweed, goldenrod, milkweed, grasses of all kinds, a cornstalk; they took them home in bundles in their arms and while the others in Bea's class were dismantling their treasures, pressing and gluing them onto construction paper with carefully copied blurbs from nature books, Claudine brought out an old crock from the basement and showed Bea how to arrange their weeds in it, russet and gold sprays, husk of the corn pulled back so it drooped like a huge yellow flower. She suggested that Bea draw the bouquet. Then, in a little booklet they'd tied with brown wool to the lip of the crock, Bea had written out stories her mother told her, remembered from Irene, about each plant in the picture.

Beatrix had been picking autumn wildflowers. To do this she'd had to brave four lanes of racing traffic and climb over a cement guard rail to reach a ravine behind the apartment where Rupert lived. She spent most of her time at Rupert's now. She stepped in the door. She had been thinking about her mother, the September beat of crickets, yellow and gold in a landscape beyond them as they walked in the pasture collecting. She had been thinking how the other kids looked at her when Claudine delivered Bea and her bouquet to school by car the day the project was due. Bea, carrying the crock carefully, had known once again she was marked. She was inventive; but somehow too much. She was someone willing to violate an agreed-upon ordinariness, her difference a betrayal as unforgivable as contempt, the bouquet, which had stood on the side shelf above the science books all week, had been tinged with the familiar sadness or loneliness every time she'd looked at it. Later a bowl of fruit stood where the crock with the corn had stood. Bea's booklet, set jauntily at its apex, instructed readers about the Florida citrus industry.

Bea took off her coat, stepped out of her rubber boots. Things her mother had taught her somehow became unavoidable barriers between Bea and others and this was the cost of living well as defined by her mother and embraced by her, and if it had not been that, separate, as Bea was, she fulfilled her mother's vision, she could not have stood it. Rupert looked at her bouquet. "Eh! Weeds!" he said.

He said it with the indulgence of a father for a little girl. Bea realized suddenly that this was how her father occasionally spoke of her mother's inventions and extravagances. She felt reduced, and then defiant. "They're *wild flowers*," she told him.

Rupert apologized. His apology too seemed an act of indulgence. She was not mollified. There was a thing some men liked to do. They liked to enjoy from a position of superiority those essential things in a woman which they would never understand. She thought of the weeds and fruit at the edge of the classroom. Perhaps it was how they coped with loneliness.

Bea's mother sent to the city all the things Bea would have been gathering for a Thanksgiving at the farm. She sent them with Liam. It was two months since Bea herself had been home. Indian corn, gourds, full corn stalks, from the field beside the yard. A pair of brass candlesticks. Her mother had assumed, correctly, that Bea would be decorating Rupert's table. She knew Bea couldn't get those things in the city, not as good and not unless she paid, something Claudine would consider extravagant. Bea wanted to send them back. In all the gifts she smelled her mother's ideal scenarios. She could also see her mother's tenderness, her need to forgive and be forgiven. She did not send them back.

Bea was in Rupert's apartment arranging when he came up behind her. His arms went around her; he kissed the side of her neck, a place she liked to be kissed. He told her that he appreciated this thing she did, and Bea thought of other tables in her mother's house. She thought of that phrase, her "special artistic touches." She was ashamed for disliking it.

The dinner went well. Bea was happy, and so was Rupert. Thanksgiving Monday she crumpled and phoned her mother. Bea told Claudine she'd missed her and talked to Henry and said she'd missed him too. It was true. She hadn't changed her mind; it was just true. Her mother's voice was careful, cautious; her father's was confused and bereft. "It's jist not the same without yer decorations," he boomed into the telephone.

Rupert's mother was also an inventor. She was a wisp with orange hair and indomitable will who, however, fell innocently under the one yoke Bea's own mother had dodged even while pretending not to: Rupert's mother had really given herself to a man, given herself away, and Claudine never had. Bea thought that Claudine maybe thought she had; she just never had. Constitutionally their mothers were different. Rupert's mother drank and there was a tragic childish gaiety about her. Each time he took Bea there to visit Bea would come away angry, confused by the dignity with which his mother nevertheless loved her life.

When they left his mother, she and Rupert would cruise in his car with the top up, fishtailing at corners in snow squalls, red vinyl flashing and the engine roaring. He had put himself permanently on the railroad sick list. They went to meet his male friends in bars, mulled beer in downtown studios over illegal wood stoves, or played pool all day. The first time Bea played pool she won two games. She realized that she'd won not just by luck but by a habit of Claudine's: projecting the paths of things, usually people, intuiting their feelings, needs, responses: it also worked with snooker balls. They went back to Rupert's place, made love, crashed and slept, rose ready for new play. Rupert smuggled scotch into concerts in the top of his cowboy boot. He strummed his guitar tentatively and sang. They smoked together far into the night, drinking more; there was a mood with him which seemed endless when they were in it or recalled it. Night would be moving into morning and they had been to the party, the bar, the speakeasy, had a tiff perhaps and gotten over it, been chilled in the car coming home and were now warming up again, and something would descend. It came with slow talk in a large dark room. Roofs and city lights stretched away from the window as they sat; a single blue candle burned on his table catching gleams from the furniture around the wall. It was his candle, but Bea had placed it. It stood aloft over ashtrays, newspapers, empty cigarette packages; they would talk in the dark, his voice swishing on and on, Bea's cracking like a counterpoint of pinging stones beside it; whiskey loosened and soothed everything in view. Their skin, their faces, the surfaces that gleamed under the candle. At some point he would reach for her. She would feel comforted and engulfed. They would sit talking still, together on his leather couch.

Bea's mother did not like leather couches. She pointed out that leather was too expensive and durable ever to re-cover, but people naturally got bored with their furniture, they needed a change. Bea had thought at the time that her mother was right, but she'd had her own reasons for disliking leather couches. Nevertheless Claudine was speaking only for herself. Claudine could not fathom anything which sought to be unchangeable.

Invention craves necessity, thought Bea. She happened to know why he got the couch. It was masculine; and it was permanent. So little was.

November came. Bea told Claudine that Rupert had asked her to live with him and that she had said yes. They might get married in a year or two if things went well.

"I'll be moving in, in a couple of weeks," said Bea.

Her mother had come into the city to visit. She was staying with Bea and they had gone out for breakfast. Her mother's eyes filled with tears. She began to pleat the blue serviette at her place, gazing down carefully. Her voice wavered as she told Bea: "You know your father and I don't approve of living together."

"I know," Bea said. "I'm sorry," unrelenting.

Claudine looked up at her. Their best speeches lay piled between them, devalued currency that no-one would exchange.

"*Why?*" her mother said.

It was the only personal thing she would allow herself.

Bea said: "We're in love."

She'd intended to say this happily or with confidence, but it came out brash. Her mother relaxed a little. Bea felt relief, realizing her mother was going to be strong. Her mother said: "You're making a big mistake. You're limiting your options."

They finished their breakfast. Bea's mother said no more. Her father, on the phone, said, "Living together seemsda be the thing to do these days," gently, in such a way that Bea would never be able to know for sure how much it had cost him to say it.

That night in Rupert's apartment they celebrated their triumph, making love in the centre of the table, pushing aside newspapers, ashtrays, dirty plates.

Part Three: Christmas

It was early December when Bea's mother next said she was coming into the city and could see her. She had come once in between, to meet a friend visiting for a conference, and had stayed in a hotel. Bea understood. Her mother was a person of principle. Neither Claudine nor Dr. Chambers had ever stayed at the homes of any of her brothers who had lived with their girlfriends. The paper cupids, the shamrocks at each place, lilies suspiring in the dark house: they were proof of different worlds. Bea met her mother at the train station. She intended to see Claudine to her hotel. She asked where it was. Her mother was turned away, collecting her little red bag on casters, untangling its pull strap. She lifted her face. Bea saw that she was drained, and sad. Claudine said, mustering a look of surprise, as if such a thing were a matter of fact, "Oh– I thought I'd be staying with you."

Bea couldn't think for a moment. "If that's all right?" her mother added.

"Of course," said Bea. She said no more. It was inconceivable that either of them should have taken advantage of this reversal. Claudine had thrown away even her principles for Bea. She meant Bea to feel privileged. Bea recognized, again, her mother's genius at work.

As it happened, and ironically, Rupert had taken a long distance train on the day of Claudine's visit. Bea was both relieved, for her mother's sake, and disappointed, for her own. They sat on the leather couch, curled up with hot chocolate after a movie. Her mother loved to see movies in the city, since the kind she liked never made it to Devonshire. Furthermore her father's labours with grounds and tractor also put him to sleep in movie theatres. They talked far into the night, as if at a pyjama party, gossiping about her brothers, their friends and girlfriends, an outing Bea's mother had taken with Henry to Irene's grave. At some point Bea caught her mother gazing at the painting above the couch. Rupert's brother had painted it, the brother with the joint as big as his finger; in it a naked, emaciated woman, lurid orange, lay curled in fetal position on an olive-drab ground. The strokes of the paint were thick, the eyes large and hollow. The long limbs were cramped inside the frame. Her mother said involuntarily: "Oh. I *don't like* that." Bea said, impervious to any ghost of Irene: "I know. I don't like it either. I'm working on him to at least get it into the back room."

They talked on. Bea put her mother to bed in the room Bea called hers and slept that night alone, happy.

Next day they spent downtown. Her mother bought Bea things. Underwear, a book Bea admired, a vase for flowers– like her own mother Claudine was of the opinion that no woman could own too many vases– a Chinese hair-clip shaped like a moth. She bought a brandy snifter for Rupert. She loaded Bea up with food, still concerned about her weight: muffins, cheeses, a package of brownies, bottles of juice. She pressed some money into Bea's hand. Bea had a meeting with a curator that would begin before her mother's train left. She was going to have to catch a streetcar to the meeting in the bleak district near the station. Claudine decided to wait with her. They stood on a corner. Glass towers leaned together above them. Nearby where a building was under construction a tall crane stood idle on its high platform. A huge tarpaulin, draped against the open side of the building, had been anchored down by hanging cables. There was a wind and the cold was growing. Snow began to fall in eddies. Flakes caught in Claudine's dark hair where the grey softened it in front.

One long taut cable began to swing in the wind. Wind caught the tarpaulin and bellied it out, and the cable slapped rhythmically against the metal strut with a long echoing sound while Bea's mother began telling her, finally, how much she was missing her. Bea never came home. The snow was falling between them. The sound of the cable rang inside the hollow strut and grew rhythmic, the beat of a heart machine in an echo chamber. Immanent goodbyes hung over them. Bea felt bereft already, reduced, unable to think of her mother going down to the train station, unable to listen.

The streetcar didn't come. Claudine had to leave to catch her train. She emptied her leftover tokens into Bea's hand and kissed and hugged her, and Bea watched her walk away, one knee stiff after last year's Christmas fall, pulling the red suitcase, until she disappeared. Bea stood on the corner without moving. The ringing sound of the blown cable beat against her. She felt the press of tears. A token dropped and she stared at it in the snow. Suddenly she remembered something. Years ago her mother had come to visit her in summer and Bea had taken her down town to see a Japanese avant-garde dance troupe give an outdoor performance. The three members of the troupe suspended themselves from the roof of a building upside down, dangling before its glass front from a spectacular height, held only by a cable attached to their ankles. Their heads were shaved and their muscular bodies were painted white; they wore muslin loincloths. To an accompaniment of echoing electronic percussion exactly like the sound of the cable in the wind, their drawn-up, tightly-balled bodies were lowered slowly into the void. Gradually they had uncurled, twisting in cryptic, cramped movements, reaching full stretch just before they touched the ground. Bea had felt exhilarated, complete; her mother had found it eerie and couldn't watch. Bea could see them now, their white bodies foetus-like descending. There were tears on her lips. A tug went deeper. Bea remembered being born. Her mother's body was contracting around her, she had a taste in her mouth like salt; it was the taste of their fluid, her first home, or it was tears. She had been warm inside there. She had not wanted to leave. She had wept in the womb, parting from Claudine.

Bea had not wanted to be born. This was Claudine's fault. Her mother should have been less. Bea stood on the corner huge, her head swishing, her heart unravelled. She felt herself back in her mother's belly, where grief and happiness had already visited her; they were pouring through her in the snow, her arms locked around chocolate and juice. The cable knocked and rang in the wind. She concluded it must be her mother's heartbeat, monitored outside on some machine. Though she'd wept being born, invention craved necessity.

Bea's painting, originally neglected out of happiness, now eluded her for other reasons. She wandered the apartment, rearranging compulsively. Her father phoned. It was almost Christmas. Her father told her that Claudine was depressed. He said anxiously: He couldn't seem to do anything to cheer her up. Would Bea come? He was diffident. Would she come early for Christmas?

He was assuming, she heard the wish in his voice, that she would come home for Christmas at all.

I don't have any money, Bea said. I can't afford the train.

Oh, I'll pay, her father said.

When her father met Bea at the train station he told her about his plan. He had explained to Claudine that he was going to pick up an early present. He had let her know a week ago that it would be coming: Claudine Chambers prided herself on her ability to guess presents and Henry liked to stump her. She had pestered him with questions. He was pleased with himself, telling Bea this. In the back of the truck sat a large box. On the seat beside him was a blanket. "We'll putja inda the box in the garage," he said, "an' I'll cover you with the blanket. She'll be so surprised."

Bea focused on the effect. She saw his glee. She saw her mother's astonishment. She agreed.

Crouched in the box she heard her mother's thin curious voice and wanted to giggle. Her mother tried guessing. A microwave? She saw Bea move. A dog?

Christmas Day her father took Bea aside and told her: Until you arrived, I'd been really discouraged about her.

Part Four: Epiphany

Christmas evening Bea went up to bed. The bathroom door was ajar and she pushed it open carelessly to brush her teeth.

Claudine was there, taking a sponge-bath. This was an archa-ism whose attraction Bea had never understood. Her mother did it when, she said, she was too tired for a shower, but Bea associated her mother's sponge-baths with Irene: when Bea's mother took a sponge-bath she was revisiting her own childhood, her mother filling the copper tub, setting it up near the stove: it was the once-a-week ritual, as the youngest Claudine took her bath last, and Irene was always there to help her wash.

Bea's mother stood now on a folded green towel naked. The sink was full and half her body was glistening. There was the deep wide swell of her belly. There were her full breasts, nipples pink-like Bea's, prominent from suckling. Across the globe of her left breast traced a long blue vein; there was her wide dark bush of hair, the smooth clear folds at thigh and groin, her slender legs, knees knobby like Bea's, her fanny vulnerable and flat, her spread knobbly feet whose toes curled quaintly up at rest. Her shoulders were round, smooth, her body short, her pale damp flesh was full of life.

Bea had known her mother's sponge-baths only by sound. Inside her pastel shy body her mother leaned in her slightly hunched way over the basin and the water purled as she dipped and wrung the green cloth. She wiped the skin of one arm. In 30 years this was how Bea's body would look. It occurred to Bea that there might be wisdom in bodies.

Back in Rupert's apartment Bea told Rupert the story of her father's plot, pleased. She was full of the glee of the successful surprise party. Rupert turned to her from the bed. He said bitterly:

"That's all you are. You're their little girl who jumps out of a box."

They were silent. Something left over hung in the room. Briefly Bea hated him. She saw that he was right and some truths were too terrible. Nobody had the right to point them out, not truths about other people's lives.

Part Five: Lent

Bea had tried to wrest some space from Rupert and though she'd done it, she had the back room as her own, she didn't know what to do there. It was too small for a studio, and anyway she already had a studio across town she rarely used. Furthermore, Rupert still thought of the room as his, her presence there a by-product of his beneficence. He'd begun to work overtime. He gave Bea to understand that her painting slump necessitated it. Bea knew this was true but she had no way of convincing him that wealth was relative. He had always made twice as much as her. Somehow, because of her, he wanted more. Somehow his wealth became her problem.

She was alone most of the time and she wandered through his apartment faster, looking for herself. What she found wiped off with a damp cloth. Things she'd anticipated had not arrived; she still couldn't name her own necessities. There were the flowers on the table, the candles and last night's dripped wax. She'd lit them alone. He was too busy for dinners. The months when he'd held her on his leather couch had given way to other things. The drinks come faster and bigger; the gravel spat; the arms, when they finally reached, were greedy. Once she had liked to cup her hand at his crotch.

Greed, or need. She had named the parts of his body. When she told him her names, her mythologizing of his skin, he hadn't understood; he'd rolled over and gone to sleep. She'd lain inventing more, his indifference a pain she was already assimilating and dismissing, the silent censure of the others in the classroom.

Next morning he told her that when he was a small child a teacher had refused to let him go to the bathroom. He'd kept asking. She'd kept denying. At last he'd wet his pants. He'd been sent home, sobbing with humiliation; his mother had told his principal and the teacher had been let go, but nothing had touched his humiliation. There had been times lately when he would have arranged Bea in bed in postures of humiliation. She wondered where his teacher was now. She twisted and fought him. He didn't like this. Or perhaps he did. Perhaps it was when fighting that he liked her, when she won and the humiliation did not take place.

She ought to get up, she ought to leave this bed.

But Claudine and Bea were inventive; Rupert necessitated so much ingenuity.

Part Six: Easter

Bea and Rupert went to a birthday party. It was in the home of wealthy friends, painters she knew who had made it; Bea had realized Rupert was overawed by artists, but the booze was high quality and there was lots of it– that would please him. The painters had a stand-up bar made of glass brick. Rupert took over the bottles lined up there, playing bartender, doing manoeuvres with the corkscrew. He grew jaunty, pouring with a flourish, cracking his characteristic awkward, oblique witticisms.

Bea's friend's husband put his hand on her back where her dress plunged. They got into a discussion about galleries. She forgot about Rupert. When she next glanced up he had found the scotch; she said something to him, about it not being served. Rupert flushed. He poured a large glassful, for himself.

"Oh, *please*," Bea said.

Her friends looked at them. Rupert sipped. His eyes became unfamiliar; he stood, his hair glowing red in the tracklights. He was waiting.

Bea ignored him. Slowly his own drama drained out of him. He seemed to wilt. Her friends were still, though Bea was thinking it must be time for the cake. Rupert said abruptly: "I knew she would never snip the umbilical chord."

Her friends turned to Bea. "Sorry," Bea said, shrugging. "He's drunk. *C'est la vie*. Shall we cut the cake?"

Her friend's husband stirred. Rupert's moment slipped. He swept the empty bottles off the bar and they clanged to the polished wood floor with a musical thud. One rolled away as he stepped towards Bea. He was no-one she knew. He stopped close in front of her.

"You're a loser," he said. "You've ruined your life. You lie to me to protect them and you're completely full of shit."

Bea hit him.

Rupert's swing was wide; it struck the back of her head and knocked her down. His boots echoed on the marble of the foyer. He had the door open. He turned. "When you think of me sacrificed for the cause of your family," he said, "repeat one word to yourself. 'Barrabas'."

The door shuddered in its frame.

"Jesus," her friends said together, and started to laugh.

Bea got up. He had succeeded, after all. He; the teacher from when he was little. Her vigilance had not been enough.

"What the hell did he mean about Barrabas?" asked her friends.

"It's one of his obscure references," Bea told them wearily. "He's styling himself as Christ, and I'm the rabble."

Neither Claudine nor Irene had to deal with humiliation. Nothing worse than a failed dessert; overheard gossip about themselves. Bea found herself breathing easily. She was on entirely new ground.

After the cake and champagne, which she actually enjoyed, she stepped out to her cab. Everything was white, a surprise late snowfall. Rupert was waiting in the cold, shivering. His face was taut and empty. Because she had gotten to know him as well as she knew her mother, Bea saw through it to some hunger wasting him. She assumed it was regret. Apologies, however, were not Rupert's style.

Nevertheless Bea knew when she deserved one. She went down to the waiting cab. When she reached to close the door he had followed.

"You with this guy?" asked the cabbie.

"No," Bea said. She closed the door quickly.

The cab pulled away. The cabbie was discreet and didn't ask why she was sobbing.

This was what happened:

Bea was alone in Rupert's apartment, where she purported to live. She was lying under the painting of the emaciated woman. She was weeping. She wept most of the time and she did not know why. She looked at the woman in the picture, her curled limbs, her hollow eyes and drawn face. She saw his mother, barefoot, mixing another martini for herself gaily. She saw her own mother, looking at the painting, saying, "Oh." She saw the woman in the painting stir. She saw her orange limbs shift and loosen. She saw the long cramped feet slip apart, the toes poke out from the canvas. The dark eyes fluttered open. Carefully, deliberately, the woman unfolded her long arms and stretched her long bony shins past the picture frame. She turned, crouching. Her luminous kneecaps rested on the edge. She narrowed her shoulders to put her arms through, and ducked her lank head. Her hair swung forward. It crackled as she slid past the sides of the frame. She stepped out onto the leather couch and down past Bea into the apartment. Her eyes burned, her hair glowed; her flexing hands, her long thin naked limbs, her skinny breasts with their shadowy nipples, ate up the dark in the centre of the room.

Unfolded, she was a giant.

Part Seven: Pentecost

Bea unlocked her studio. There was dust everywhere. She sat on a stool which was no longer familiar to her, and looked out the window. The view was industrial.

She had left the door ajar. Idly she imagined Claudine standing in it. She saw her there, looking around with the trepidation of those unsure about the paraphernalia of art. Then Claudine's eyes lit on the dirt. Her face grew confident. She breathed in. "Pooh! It's stuffy in here!" she exclaimed. "Won't the windows open, dear?"

Bea turned to the window to slide it back. It gave with a thud. Spring air poured through the aperture and she sat watching it as if it were visible, covering her skin, the dust, crusted brushes, turpentine rags, spare stretchers, old boards, an easel, canvases with their faces against the wall. The air was green mist. The light in the studio had gone chartreuse. Bea picked up the nearest rag. It was part of their attention to beauty that they were good at cleaning when they chose to be.

Part Eight: The Season of Ordinary Time

Claudine had made lunch and she stood in the farm kitchen behind the counter. She was waiting for Bea. When Bea came in she could tell that her mother had been waiting because the circles under her eyes were darker than usual, there was an awareness in how her knuckles rested on the counter. But her mother smiled, a smile which did not reach the tension in her eyes. The table was set. Bea slung her bag over a chair. She sat in the chair, which was not at either of the two set places. Two rose place-mats; Irene's good china and silver and the napkins Claudine sewed from a length of chintz she'd found in Irene's things after she died. In the centre a kerosene lamp, spring flowers from the garden. Claudine look at Bea.

"Your father has Rotary today," she said.

Automatically they thought of him there: speaking the arcane language of men's clubs, refuelling for another week. Claudine came round the counter and embraced Bea where she sat. Her mother lit the lamp. Bea started to cry.

She cried silently. She did not sob. It was no good. Her mother cried the same way Bea did. Bea had her face in her hands. Bea knew them both. They were both tired.

Then Bea told her mother what her mother already expected to hear, that she would be leaving Rupert, and Claudine started to cry too; and, in the track of one tear down her mother's cheek Bea saw that Claudine had erased all her former advice to Bea against him. They hovered, near her mother's table: at some table, perhaps bigger than her mother's. Bea cried because she was sorry for herself and because it was necessary to cry over love. Her mother cried because a union had ended.

After a while they sat at their places. They wiped their tears at the same time. Noticing this they laughed, and then they were suddenly hungry. Claudine poured them wine.

When Henry came in he cried "Wall what's going on here?", glad to see Bea but preparing to be alarmed, and her mother answered as they both kissed him,

"Oh, girl talk."

The Names of Horses

Bea asked her parents, Would they say they were country people or town people? (She did not say "city." City didn't enter into it.) "Country," said Mrs. Chambers comfortably.

"Hick," boomed her father from the rocking chair. "I'm a hick. Not that it's a bad thing. I'm proud of it." And he leapt up, a way he had of jumping with mysterious concentration from one topic to another allowing no discernible transition, to put a second log on the fire.

Bea's father was going deaf. Because he was a doctor he had postulated a cause: target practice with a shotgun, but no ear-plugs, when he was a boy. How old? Bea's father, nine or twelve. He was lifting the gun thicker than his leg-bone, he was squeezing the trigger with a clumsiness never quite smoothed out in later life. The pony started where it stood between the shafts of the highjacked cutter and the gun's explosion rocked somewhere far inside Henry Chambers' ears the seed of a family now gone to jungle around them: Bea's mother, him, Bea, her brothers, their wives, the grandchildren, his brother, his sisters: a world that greened with less and less sound thanks to a shotgun, and no earplugs, when he was a boy.

"Nerve damage," said Dr. Chambers. He said it slightly loudly and with no trace of self-pity. He was sitting in his spot at the kitchen table, a spot he never varied and from which he could look out the window at their fields. Bea imagined that the tears— which since the accident found it easier to arrive at his eyes— would swim up next. But they didn't. He cried remembering his dead father and mother, he cried remembering his dead mare, his dead wolfhound, the years of his practice when he came home only to collapse into bed for a few hours and so missed knowing his children. He cried sometimes when they were all together at holidays, laughing, making black-humoured supercilious jokes and talking, debating politics or human relations or art in fiercely intellectual terms he couldn't himself sustain nor cared too. He cried once when Mrs. Chambers' brother was unkind to her. But he never cried for himself.

"Oh- " he would often say, a dismissive, jaunty wave of one hand. His hands were like mitts, the fingers short and thick as overstuffed sausages. They had given him away at a costume party once when a patient had recognized them. "I leave all the intellectual stuff to your mother"- and grinned, pleased at having invented a new form of hookey.

His older brother Luther always held his hand and in turn he always led him, impatient and foolhardy, into escapades. They would be sent to school or to Bible class and Henry would come up with better things to do- fish, shoot peas at people going into church- and once these ideas were carried out, Bea's uncle would always feel responsible. From the beginning they were trying to liberate each other: Bea's uncle from her father's waywardness, crooked cap and grin, her father from her uncle's seriousness, his confident and sad, carefully erect posture. After such adventures there would sometimes be beatings and each waited tensely through the other's turn; Mrs. Chambers liked to say darkly that Bea's father had had the imagination strapped out of him, but her father himself spoke of his own father, who had introduced the razor strap with regret and Methodist theology, only in terms of love. It was a love Henry Chambers believed to have been returned. "Father would always say, 'This- hurts- me- more than it hurts- you,'" Dr. Chambers would tell them, in the measured and emphasized singsong he used for recollections. Bea, listening to this explanation, would be overcome with the scepticism of her age, which she believed a more enlightened one than her father's: she would identify and tag in her grandfather's reputed speeches, Victorian Machismo, Justification by Self-Righteousness, The Christian Patriarchy in Full Flight. Her female cousins said to her in their own peculiar ringing tones: "Grandfather Chambers would be considered a *child-abuser* now Bea, *no question* about it," and then subsided, glowering, leaving Bea to wonder about things: how in spite of certain bearable complaints their parents– Bea's father, her cousins' mother– their uncle, were all right; how they themselves were all right; how it was still true about their grandfather's capacity to love; how Bea herself had doted on him until he died. If the previous male generation, composed of Henry and Luther, were to be believed, they had grown up feeling none the worse and perhaps even a little closer, for her grandfather's disciplinary sessions in the woodshed.

The brothers had been separated finally by Henry's pleurisy. It was during the war. Bea's father, rejected for active service, began local undercover work for the RCMP instead while her uncle finished medical training with the Canadian forces. Luther went overseas and spent his time patching up, rather than killing people. Henry yawned in the back rows of German-Canadian Club meetings, ostensibly alert for seditious activity. When questioned about this now, Dr. Chambers would say "It was jist a bunch of old farmers worried about gitting by," and wave one hand; if pressed he might purse his lips, mutter in a deprecating way still redolent with fifty-year-old boredom, "Half a them useda fall asleep." His expression, deadpan, would turn gleeful. He affected to find his war contribution funny. There was also in his recollections something equally typical: a belief they were irrelevant simply because they were past. Bea believed this attitude masked disappointment. In the RCMP her father had hoped to learn horseback riding, and instead they had made him muck stalls and clean tack before turning him into a spy.

They had a few pictures of the war years. Bea's Uncle Luther looked more upright, more responsible, more elegant than ever; her father, Clark Gable mustache and Mountie stripes, looked raffish and irrepressible, the danger he radiated strictly sexual in nature. Only in respective wedding pictures did the brothers suddenly become similar: Luther stood by a flight of church steps in his army uniform, while his diminutive bride leant, beautiful as a film star, on the railing just above him; her father, engulfed in baggy suit and greatcoat and fedora, looked, slightly dazzled, into her mother's large tear filled eyes. Both men seemed tentative and a bit lost: cautiously hopeful despite their youth and brawn.

Bea's father would miss all this and focus on his feet in the photograph. "Oh say lookit there," he'd cry, pointing. "There's your Uncle Luther's shoes. I'd gone and forgot mine back at the hotel!" Bea would look at the black toes of her father's brogues and then back at the wives. They were women, even so young, who exuded power. Her aunt's was a core of steel; her mother's was less conscious, the brazen confidence of the virgin whose lust is for motherhood. Bea knew that in photographs after the war a new balance had evolved between the brothers. There were few photographs of her uncle after the war. Whenever Luther and his wife came to visit they would have to leave again shortly, because, they said, the wildness of the Chambers' human traffic made them dizzy.

She often wondered what, if anything, lay between her Uncle Luther's elegance and her father's homespun profligacy. What did it mean to Luther that her father had seven sons and Bea, while Luther had no children at all? Her uncle's elegance concealed a careful, loving and loyal soul. Under her father's mad bounty lay more of the same. They had come together over the years because of their mutual love of horses, cemented long ago in cart or cutter when they set off as boys driving towards misadventure. Now, since the accident, there was something else: in both of them a delving into roots, a rekindling of the old brotherly responses; in her father a longing for acknowledgement, for appreciation, which could sometimes cross the line into truculence.

Lately his conversation with Bea was peppered with oblique complaints.

"When I think now of how hard I worked when you guys

were young, I don't know how I- "

"I suggested we visit the Bottomses but no, your mother was too busy, and now Mr. Bottoms has had a coronary- "

"I put a new base on the hitching post. It was your Uncle Luther's idea. Your mother didn't think it needed one, she said it was a waste of time, but don't you think it looks better?"

"People sure must like my wine. Three litre-and-a-half bottles of it gone this weekend- "

When Dr. Chambers spoke this way Bea would try with a sort of fierce merriness to reassure him. It might once have been forced merriness; but somewhere inside, Bea had discovered her mother's confidence. In Bea it alternated between awful sympathy and irrepressible humour.

"That's what you get. If your wine weren't so good, nobody would drink it."

"You did work hard. We wouldn't be who we are without you."

"Dad, that hitching post looks a *lot* better!"

She would take his hand. His mottled sausage fingers would swallow hers. They were the same hands: hers miniature, thinner, but their relation still obvious. "Gramma had hands like this, Dad?" she would ask; she took sly but intense pleasure in reminding him of things he loved. His face would soften; he would grow bemused. Tears would start up. "Yep. ...Mother's ...hands," he would murmur. "Mother had the shortest, stubbiest fingers in the world. Pudgy." This would lead him to some decisive medical fact. "Mother was always overweight." He would sit, squeezing Bea's fingers shyly. Bea would squeeze back.

The others grew impatient with his truculence. Now that she no longer lived at home Bea had begun to suffer a kind of pain over this on her father's behalf. She redoubled her efforts to include him, aware of their obviousness and not caring. By contrast her mother, when fed up, would ignore him, defend herself against his complaints, or walk out of rooms; later she would tell Bea: "All I said was he had that dresser he was wanting to refinish before Christmas, and now he's got it in his head I said the new hitching post was a *bad idea*." Her mother would expel a breath, exasperated. She and Bea would have a talk in which Bea tried delicately to suggest that, alone in a sea of offspring not one of which was like him, Dr. Chambers perhaps was feeling the need for reassurance and inclusion. Her mother, always kind and sensible when not under attack, would agree. Then Bea would pause, draw back, consider their conversation, asking herself if such exchanges in some subtle way demeaned them. Dr. Chambers had inherited his struggles. The abstraction and objectivity his family lived in as their natural element, their relative skill with emotions, their quick low pattering voices, eddied around him while he fought alone, an isolated Hercules, on the front lines of self-knowledge. Dr. Chambers sometimes now betrayed regret for flaws he saw he'd had; tears would swim into his eyes and he would leave the table suddenly, headlong as always, believing himself invisible, to blow his nose in the pantry.

Since the accident, Time had also changed. For Bea at least and she suspected also for him, Time had become a pressing and finite thing, the length of even an aggravating life too short for sacrifices that left bitterness. Bea believed the message of her father and uncle to be, in the end, that her father was innocent: he was not intellectual, he was free of ulterior motives; he didn't know what he provoked and when. He was the most honest one among them. He liked horses because they were quiet and put no conditions on affection; they reminded him of the days before responsibility arrived. From the back of a horse he could sometimes see beyond the reach of his vast family. Solid on his white mare, limpid, muffled in growing silence, he battled on.

Dr. Chambers' recent suffering was a hazy memory. He considered it, if asked, with an expression on his face compounded of awe and bemusement: as if the most amazing thing, more amazing than his recovery from the brink of death, was that it had happened to him. He hadn't heard the stable girl's shouts. The filly had been white-eyed to the sky when she hit his horse where he sat looking at the bean field. He and the white mare dropped onto last year's dun stalks like a split container falling onto a pier. His head smacked the post of the runway gate. Two geldings that stood with noses over the rail started back in alarm. The mare snorted as the wind went out of her and lunged to her feet again, hooves scrabbling briefly among the dead beanstalks, as his boots pulled free from the stirrups. The filly raced off through the pale rows towards the sideroad. The stable girl came unglued from the barn door. His mare stood over him, lipping at his corduroys. Inside the runway the geldings moved cautiously forward to snuffle his broken glasses.

He was bleeding, the stable girl told Bea later. His nose and mouth, an' is ears. From'is *ears*.

Bea had come in from an appointment with a psychiatrist to find a message on her phone machine. It was her mother's voice. Her mother's voice always sounded thin and vulnerable on phone machines; now it shook, pausing, at one point, over a near-break into tears.

"Hello, Beatrix. I'm phoning to tell you your father's had an accident. They've taken him to Toronto by ambulance. I don't want you to worry, dear... it *is* serious..." She paused. "...but they say it isn't– life-threatening."

Bea began to feel cold. Her mother went on, thready but not crying: "Jeffrey and Diane are at the hospital now. If you could join them right away that would be the best thing." She meant Bea's brother and his wife who lived in Toronto. "I'm leaving the farm now with Arthur and Cathy and the girls."

Uppermost in Bea's mind was the need to know how old her father was. 70? 71? She saw him at his last birthday party in July, grinning, his lips rounded into an exaggerated 'O' over a gift made by one of the children. He was saying appropriate things in his singsong voice, also used for exclamations at present-givings and to disguise his reluctance in any sort of limelight. Candles tilted drunkenly in an approaching cake, carrot because as he told anyone who would listen "It was nothing but chocolate, chocolate, chocolate the whole time you guys were growing up,

gooey chocolate faces, gooey chocolate fingers on the furniture,
I am *sick* a chocolate." Their voices, stilled briefly from jokes and
polemic, joined on different keys singing Happy Birthday. She
had thought of birth. A day. Years ago her father arrived while
Luther waited eagerly, anticipating the end of loneliness, outside
her grandmother's bedroom door; now he listed stiffly over the
candles crying out mock protests and blew with a luffing noise
to impress his grandson. Behind him in the apple trees a robin's
trilled notes dropped into the dark. Gold porch light spilling over
his shoulder lost itself between the trunks. At the feet of the trees
the dewing grass stretched silver. 70 or 71?

Bea made it to the hospital.

Jeff was relieved to see her. Diane had been guarding coats
alone in the waiting room beside a young prisoner in institutional
greens attached to a guard by a set of handcuffs. The prisoner
had a black eye and his knuckles were wrapped in gauze. Jeff
joined Diane gratefully, leaving Bea by her father's bed. It was
not a bed really. It was a wheeled stretcher. They were in a side
room of the emergency ward. An intercom blared from the wall
and nurses wandered in and out, looking at charts on clipboards,
complaining about coffee breaks; there was equipment by her
father's bed which Bea didn't recognize, all of it chrome and
wheeled for silent movement. In the next bed an elderly gentle-
man was begging for help in a cracked voice. Bea's father couldn't
hear him. It turned out the old man needed to pee. Bea handed
him a bottle, and the rest of the time she did not budge from the
rail of her father's bed. She stood upright, his cold sausage fingers
in hers, and this was where Mrs. Chambers and Arthur found
her when they emerged from rush hour traffic five hours later.

What Bea never did escape was blood. The memory of it hung
between her and her father whenever she saw him; it remained
there regardless of how long they were together. She held her
father's hand. She talked to him about wine, horses, hitching
posts, about Uncle Luther's new dressage mare. She flung the
saddle over some borrowed horse boarding in the stable, tight-

ened the girth, rode to find him, leant down to speak loudly to him over the sound of the chain-saw where he stood by a pile of firewood, she called him from under the raised hood of the tractor where he droned, searching through mechanical parts, she delivered messages from her mother while he struggled with wire at the pasture fence, and there was blood on his face in the emergency room. She had stood alone, staring down an old connection abruptly nullified. His head had collided with a gate post. The family had been brought beyond what they knew. Her father had always had the strength and health of a draft-horse and now the unexpected had arrived and it was the actual frailty of a life; it was the mutability of skin or bone, of a moment when one may sit on a white mare looking at a bean field which swoops into autumn. Bea knew that her revelation was not unique; the stable girl, her mother, Arthur and his family, Jeffrey and Diane, had already had it today and so had everyone who passed through the emergency ward and so had the doctors, the invisible surgeons, x-ray technicians, medical students, the nurses, the prisoner in the waiting room, they lived with it daily: for those left, those still innocent, it was just a matter of time. Nature asserted herself. By nature Bea now understood not only the biology of chlorophyll but something vaster, the humbling, unseen cosmology by which another's life remains his own despite any amount of love.

One temple was slightly caved in. Blood scabbed darkly on it and ran under the skin in both eye sockets; his eyes and the bridge of his nose had turned purple. One eyelid was swollen shut. Swelling drew a featureless line from ear to jaw to shoulder. Once a medical resident came to shine a light in her father's pupils; when he pulled up the battered lid Bea saw an unrecogniz-able object, glistening, engorged, bright red, with a grey blot at its centre. Blood had caked in her father's thick coarse silver hair. Someone had tried to wash a little of it off, leaving the spiked hairs there stained yellow; elsewhere in his hair the blood had dried and was now flaking. A clear plastic tube taped below his nostril ran from his nose to a machine. The machine gave off the broken crackle-hum-crackle of suction interrupted by fluid as dark red bubbles slid lazily back and forth in the tube's curve. Fluid sounded in his throat when he breathed.

Another tube ran to an intravenous needle in the back of his hand. The black rubber band of a blood pressure cuff circled his arm above the elbow; under his farm tan he had gone whitish yellow. Bea bent and kissed him. The smell of blood on his breath, in the tube from his stomach, had a taint like spoiling meat. When she straightened she saw inside the curve of his ear a pooled and hardened black mass from which darker runnels had streamed into the creases of his neck and dried.

He opened his eyes briefly.

"Hello dear," he said weakly, in the same tones he would use to welcome her home for a holiday. "How are you feeling?"

He was referring to her mental health. He knew about the psychiatrist. Bea's heart made a circuit of her chest and lodged in her throat. She said clearly and loudly: "*Much* better."

He nodded once, the judicious nod with which he tended to receive facts relating to someone's health. The tubes tightened briefly and sagged again. A few bubbles of blood gurgled past his nostril. She knew a moment of satisfaction for having managed to speak loud enough. He murmured again.

"Pardon Dad?"

"Are you going riding this weekend?"

Uncle's Luther's horse was named Mack. He was a thoroughbred and had some other elaborate name, required amongst horse owners to record lineage and impress show judges and each other, but Bea always forgot it. On the rare occasions in her childhood when the Chambers had piled into a station wagon to visit, Bea inevitably found herself in the stable with her father and Uncle Luther while her uncle, turned out in his still-good army breeches, would lecture them about Mack and about the care of horses in general. Bea's uncle was the undisputed horseman in the family. He had ridden in the army, taken to it, studied it, and later paid for lessons in the invisible arts of

dressage. His horses, schooled and showed by national equestrian stars, had done respectably at high level competitions.
Those members of the family interested in horses, which meant
Bea and her female cousins, found her uncle's knowledge slightly
intimidating; added to it, he had the clipped exact delivery of one
who had spent time in the army. Nevertheless, in the end they
saw Uncle Luther's horses as an extension of himself: subtle if
formal, impeccably trained, gentle despite their size.

Her uncle would put Mack on the long lunge line and lead
him out to the paddock. He would chirp at Mack with brittle
love and Mack would unfold his black legs, bow his black head
slightly, reply with a canter as careful, graceful and precise as her
uncle's voice. For Bea there was the power her uncle's voice
controlled; there was the alien soldierliness she had once mis-
taken for disapproval; there was the terrible suspense his voice
set up in her waiting for the release of its music. Even now when
she thought of Luther's voice she felt surprise: as if at some
unexpected gesture of diplomacy.

Once the child Bea and her father were in her uncle's barn
Bea would be offered a ride she hadn't the fortitude either to
welcome or refuse. She would swing herself into the saddle. This
would impress her uncle inordinately and so make her slightly
less timid– he always expected she would need a leg-up to the
back of a horse whose shoulder stood level with her head. Her
toes would nose instinctively for the stirrup-bars. She would settle
her black velvet helmet, brim cracked from a fall; she would
gather the reins up, threading them through her third and little
fingers and out the tops of her fists. Bea had been six when her
father first hefted her onto the new bay farm pony and trotted
her round the side driveway in front of their barn. Though not
naturally athletic her muscles had eventually recorded things.
Now Luther considered her a rider of potential, a situation she
found both flattering and alarming, like receiving some costly pet
she hadn't asked for.

From the top of Uncle Luther's horse Bea could see all across
her aunt's blooming garden. She could see over the stone wall

to the back of the house, over the white paddock fence to a maze of green fields. The stable, also white, sat beside the paddock. Next to it, his foot on the bottom rung of the gate, her father leaned into the sun. At the centre of it all stood her uncle with the red line in his hand, and revolving around him in concentric circles obedient to his commands, ran his bay horse and Bea.

"Terrrr-ot!" sang out her uncle. Mack sprang off his fetlocks into a long float and the green world spun round Luther's voice. Bea set her chin and sank into the soughing of her uncle's carefully-oiled saddle; her legs found the grooves from his legs, she tried to become the vessel that he wanted, receptor for sound flown along the line into the horse and her. Mack's dark sides gleamed. His carefully trimmed mane fluttered up. He snorted without disturbing the perfect set of his head and carried her forward and up as the bright air swept by them. The horse's great height was mostly leg. Without leaving her uncle, her father, her aunt's garden, Bea and Mack moved as if from planet to planet in strides a mile long.

"Follow with your back," sang her uncle, "that's the way now." Then "Up-up-up! Head up! Eyes forward, get those heels down!" Mack's shoes clicked against stones in the paddock dirt. Bea tried to think simultaneously of all parts of her body. Her heels jammed past the stirrup-bars, her back rolled to the horse's gait, her thighs clung with the upward lift of the saddle. "Don't drop that inside shoulder now," said her uncle. "Shoulder up! Now prepare to canter. Follow, follow, follow." His voice stopped and Mack's heat closed around her. They hurtled forward. "And," said her uncle gently, "ca-a-a-a-a-n-ter!" Mack began to rock. "Get your horse on the bit now," her uncle said, "get him collect-ed, quar-ters un-der." Her hips tilted. "That's it," said her uncle. "C'mon Mackie, get up there." He clucked. Mack's body rolled under her, the flash of his long legs reaching past his shoulder receded from view. They rocked. "A-a-a-nd halt," said her uncle, and Mack rocked once more and stopped dead as softly as a flower falling from its stem. Bea leaned forward slightly, straight-ened, and was still. The fields flattened themselves. Dr.

Chambers' face swam into focus by the gate. In his proud smile Bea saw that he had relinquished her without rancour. At the same time, she felt his anticipation with relief: soon Luther's day would be done and her father, when she climbed down from the horse, would have her back again. "How'd you enjoy that?" Dr. Chambers asked rhetorically. He asked with enthusiasm, innocent of the longing in his voice, devoid of any envy. He added for Luther's benefit: "Say, isn't Mack a beautiful horse?!"

"He's great," said Bea.

Her uncle clapped Mack's neck. "There, pet," her uncle sang out. She swung her leg over the cantle and dropped to the ground. Mack looked round at her. She rubbed his black forehead under his brow-band. Dr. Chambers swung the gate open and the horse walked free back to the stable, long-legged and loose, head and reins swinging, tail swishing, and the three of them followed.

Every ten minutes Bea's father shifted restlessly. With colds and flu's he had always been a bad patient, and on birthdays and Father's Day he never, unlike her mother, wanted breakfast in bed. "Patients eat in bed," he would say. "I want mine at a table." Now he looked under his one good lid for Bea. "Are they going to aspirate?" he murmured. "Have I seen an orthopod yet?"

"They're waiting for the CT room, Dad. You have to have a scan."

He didn't seem to digest this. "Have they done x-rays?"

"Yes."

The resident came in again. He was young and handsome and he hung over the bed rail across from Bea gracefully, talking about Dr. Chambers' broken skull. It was broken in several places. The eye socket was also broken. A piece of skull lay against his brain, which had bled. "Now we watch him. We gauge his memory loss. But we can't assess permanent damage for a long time," the resident told her in his opaque Ethiopian accent. "The CT scan will show us the extent of the clot under his fractures."

He smiled at Bea sympathetically with dark chocolate eyes. He had been told that his patient was also a doctor. He said to her father: "Hello, sir, can you tell me your name please?"

Dr. Chambers shrugged weakly. He pursed his lips. Bea saw immediately that he had not comprehended. She said swiftly, "He's hard of hearing. Sometimes if a response doesn't make sense it's because he hasn't heard."

The resident thanked her. "I also have a very thick accent," he offered disarmingly. "Is one ear better than the other?"

"No," said Bea.

The resident leaned closer.

"Can you tell me your name, sir?"

"Henry Chambers."

"Do you know what happened to you?"

"Fell off my horse, I giss."

"And do you know where you are?"

"Hospital," said her father matter-of-factly.

"Can you tell me what year it is?"

He seemed to search. The effort exhausted him in a second; he shrugged and seemed to go to sleep.

"Dr. Chambers? Can you tell me what year it is?"

Her father murmured faintly, stiff with embarrassment but proud: "1943."

The resident turned to Bea smoothly. "By 'aspirate' he must have meant any clot on his brain," he told her, projecting sympathy. "But if a patient is over age 30 we're not so quick to intervene surgically in head injuries." Still relaxed, he started to leave. "I can be more useful upstairs, putting pressure on the CT people."

Bea adjusted her father's sheet. She was worried about him feeling cold. She herself was freezing. After another half hour her father said abruptly: "Where's Claudine?"

"On her way," said Bea. "With Arthur and Cathy and the girls. Jeffrey and Diane are in the waiting room. Liam will be here after his night class."

"All here, are you?" he asked faintly, surprised, eyes closed.

"Of course," said Bea, though by "all" they could mean only family living in Ontario. "We care about you, you know."

The pressure of his fingers in hers tightened a little. A clot of blood choked and then whooshed down the tube. "What's this tube doing?" he asked. "Draining my stomach?"

"I guess so."

An hour passed. Bea listened to his pained breathing and the sounds of the tube.

"I'm tryna remember," her father said suddenly, "the names of our horses. Those ponies. I forgit the names a those ponies."

The Chambers had started with not one but two farm ponies. Their names were Corgi and Bounder. Small bay geldings of indeterminate breeding, they scraped Bea and her cousins off under thorn trees or against fences, lay down on the barn floor when the saddle was put on, or held their breaths for the tightening of the girth so that later when you put your foot in the stirrup the saddle would slide down to their bellies. After her father had trotted her around the side drive Bea had picked up the basics of reining; Dr. Chambers assured her with character-istic cheerful lack of sympathy that the rest she would learn by falling off a lot. From these inauspicious beginnings Bea and her best girlfriend Charlene, who lived up the road, began their years of obsessive horseback riding. Without benefit of riding lessons or even much parental supervision, they trotted, with the oblivi-ous courage of seven-year-olds, around the side paddock after school and sometimes cantered, maybe even twice, arms, legs and braids flapping, up the lane from the pond. Then Charlene's father bought her a pony of her own. It was a tiny perfect chestnut with snapping eyes and a sleek mincing gait, and he also bought her a new saddle, child's size, and a bridle, and enrolled her in lessons. Charlene trotted her new pony, whose name was Coco, down the two miles of concession to visit Bea. Her new saddle was low and small and uncomplicated. The bit on her new bridle had rings at the sides and a pretty, if superfluous, brown noseband. Charlene herself wore a black velvet helmet with a professional-looking cup for her chin on the strap. She tossed her long blonde hair.

"I ride *English*," she told Bea.

Bea looked at Bounder. He stood somnambulant, one rear hock cocked, lids half-lowered over his blue wall-eyes, his head inclined genially towards the mud. She examined the high cantle of the saddle, the large horn for anchoring roped steers, the enormous flaps which covered the stirrups to protect the rider's toes from sagebrush. Charlene's new pony pawed the ground and extended her nose, snorting. Bounder looked back at her and she squealed loudly and ejected a stream of milky pee from under her raised tail. "She's in heat," said Charlene importantly. "I better keep 'er away." The pony wheeled in a circle and they were gone. Bea watched the low spurts of gravel: already Charlene stuck to her pony's back like a burr.

Bea threw Bounder's reins over the mailbox and went into the house. Her mother was in the kitchen basting a chicken, dressed for some meeting in town. It seemed to Bea that Claudine Chambers spent most evenings of their childhoods attending meetings: church Council, United Church Women, the Library Board, Board of Education; usually, she left complicated notes for Bea or her brothers and it was them who got supper. "Is Dad home?" Bea asked her.

"Try the basement dear, why?"

Bea clumped downstairs. Her father was bent over the workbench in his favourite beige coveralls. Underneath the coveralls he still wore his shirt and tie from seeing patients and he was decanting homemade wine from a giant vat that stood on the floor. "Lookit- Beatrix," he said, "jist hold that tube up while I git the suction going, will you?" Handing Bea a loop of plastic hose he put one end in the vat and the other in his mouth and began to suck. Bea watched silently as red wine crept up the hose. Her father pinched the end near his mouth; swallowed; and stuck the tip into the first of a row of clean wine bottles that stood on the work bench. He worked for some time, filling the bottles. "Dad," said Bea. "Charlene has an English saddle."

"Does she?" He pinched the hose, lifted the other end out of the vat, and drank off the wine in the tube. "I don't want to ride Western any more." He began to cap up the wine bottles. "Say I think there's an old army flat-saddle of your Uncle Luther's in the granary," he told her. "Let's just finish this wine."

The saddle was huge, dusty, and stiff with cobwebs. She spent evenings with it perched on a sawhorse in the barn, rubbing neet's-foot oil into the leather according to Uncle Luther's instructions while barn cats twirled around her ankles. Thereafter she circuited the paddock alone, bouncing precariously on the old saddle, somehow oblivious that it was uncomfortable and far too large. If her father had gotten through his patients early he would occasionally stop his car at the end of the paddock near the road and watch, grinning through the rolled-down window and calling encouragement. She had assimilated the departure of her friend Charlene. She rode by herself with her usual clumsy seven-year-old's concentration.

One day in spring Dr. Chambers came to Bea where she sat curled in the window drawing horse's heads. In those days Bea's only signature on school work was the stylized hieroglyph of a horse.

"How'dja like a new pony?" Dr. Chambers asked her portentously and without preamble. Bea looked up at him. When she was older she would be able to identify what she saw in his face: eagerness; the wild hope of a boy with a new plan for mischief.

"Corgi and Bounder," said Bea. "The farm ponies."

"Corg and Bounder," Dr. Chambers said. A nurse arrived, smiled coolly at Bea, and took his pulse and blood pressure. "Hello sir," she said, "can you hear me?" Bea told her to speak louder. "What is your name?" called the nurse.

"Bounder had a wall-eye."

"Two wall-eyes," said Bea.

The nurse repeated her question.

"Henry Chambers," murmured her father, rolling his good eye open a crack.

"Can you tell me where you live?"

"On a farm."

"And how old are you?"

"Oh let's see. Sev'ndy? Sev'ndy-one? Sumpm like that anyhow." He shut his eye with finality. The nurse went away. Another half hour passed. "There was Corgi and Bounder," he said to Bea suddenly. "Then Duchess. That grey pony. Then... Was it... Roo?" He lapsed into silence.

The soles of Bea's feet turned rubbery. The resident came to fetch him for the CT scan. She asked him when the neurosurgeon would arrive and when he said the neurosurgeon had to wait for the scan results she told him her father was worse. "Corgi... " said her father. The tube crackled and a chain of red drops poured down its curve. "Bounder... Luther... Duchess... You'll be wanting yer dinner now. D'you know the way out?"

Duchess came to them aged and dignified by half a dozen foals. She wore the dainty dished face of the Welsh pony and had a Welsh pony's large soft dark eye; she also had the mysterious distinction of having been trained for the pony sulky races. She was never happier than when she stood in the snow between the traces of the cutter. Bea's father had bought the cutter at a barn auction somewhere and rigged it up with red paint and bells; each time Bea settled the saddle on Duchie's grey back she could tell that the pony had been hoping instead for the straps of a harness, and when she pushed her into a trot she was longing for a stretch of track. It was nearly impossible to get Duchess to canter. When pressed, she would only trot faster.

On a bright morning a strange trailer pulled into the Chambers' side yard. Bea ran outside as Duchess's small black hooves skittered down from it into the driveway; Duchess lifted her muzzle and the white of her dark eye rolled, she snorted emphatically, and she was still. Bea's father put her into the stall where in anticipation Bea had shaken out a bed of straw two feet deep. Bea peered at her as she snuff led her feedbox and her window. Dr. Chambers stood beside Bea, admiring. "She's- a beautiful– conformation– little mare," he said, full of pleasure. They stood not touching. Slightly preoccupied and clumsy he rattled a juice tin of oats into the pony's bin and stood back again. "Duuuuu-cheee," Bea crooned. Duchess's head swung up and her wide grey forehead came round, her shell-shaped ears pricked forward. "Duuu-chee." The pony waded through the straw and blew at them. Bea and her father stepped forward together, two hands reaching for the pink snip on her nose.

Christmas time her father and brothers hauled the cutter out of the drive shed. They bundled up under a plaid blanket, features hidden in toques and ear muffs and oversized mitts, and her father driving, Duchess trotting out while steam-clouds poured from her flared scarlet nostrils, they sped up the road to the swamp and back. The bells jingled; the buff and white winter ditches, dark trunks of bare maples flew by. Winter light slanted over them sideways. Her father clucked, holding the long reins. "Luther and I useda drive da school in winter," he told Bea happily.

Bea's family took over the waiting room on the floor of the hospital devoted to neurosurgery patients. Dr. Chambers had lapsed into broken consciousness and his bed now stood among a vast array of machines in Intensive Care. Entry to Intensive Care was controlled and guests had to beep the nurses through an intercom in the waiting room to request permission to enter; visitors were restricted to two at a time, a rule the Chambers inevitably broke. Beside their father an elderly woman with a hose inserted through a hole in her throat choked in an upright chair. Sometimes the mechanical bellows which kept her breathing would begin to beep and the old woman's nurse would come over, painfully slowly Bea thought, to vacuum out hose and throat with a suction gadget installed in the wall by the bellows. Every patient had a personal Intensive Care nurse. As nurses went they seemed a breed unto themselves: quiet, alarmingly efficient, tending to coolness, brazenly calm. Bea felt both grateful to them and slightly intimidated. She could not imagine being quite so unmoved by the extremes of pain, injury, and decay which made up their working lives.

On Dr. Chambers' other side lay a young woman grown obese from six months in a coma. Expensively dressed parents came every day and sat with the young woman, calling her name lovingly, rubbing her legs, recounting bits of news from a life she was not living; on screens next her bed green lines showed the minimal activity of a body in suspension. Dr. Chambers's own heartbeat sent a blipping green line up and down his video screen. His brain waves jigged along an adjacent monitor and cables led from these units to flat metal disks taped on his body. Sometimes they would watch their father's obsessive if whispered hospitality- "Have y'eaten yet?" "Wall, you'll be tired now, timeda go home"- translated into leaping static. So far, the clot in his brain had not moved. It was neither being absorbed nor growing worse. The bruising in his face spread through his cheeks and neck and his other injuries continued to stabilize while his doctors continued to wait. It sometimes gave Bea and her brothers an eerie feeling to know that had their father been young he would already have had brain surgery; out on the ward the Chambers would pass post-operative patients distinguished by a vast head bandage shaped like a ziggurat. Bea began to call it the "silo-roof bandage." Those who were not wearing one had heads partially or wholly shaved, and marks of old incisions showing dark through the stubble; they hauled themselves haltingly back and forth along the hall rail, frequently cheerful. Their cheerfulness was unexpected, and the Chambers took it as a sign of the relative invincibility of the human spirit. In the case of immobile patients who showed no feeling at all- old women in chairs, a teenage boy with tattoos and black t-shirt who drooled- it was their families instead who remained cheerful. Parents and lovers arrived shortly after breakfast, chirruping, burbling news, steeled against silence and sympathetic stares. Siblings, cousins, and friends came at lunch or for evening visiting hours to gossip over boxes of chocolates and silver message-balloons. HANG IN THERE. KEEP SMILING. GET

WELL SOON. As time went on, the stream of people visiting unresponsive patients would trickle down to mothers and girlfriends. They were always women of a particular sort: tireless, with a demanding belief in miracles, who seemed to evoke tears even as they repudiated their own.

The Chambers came to recognize stages in a family's readjustment. Patients arrived on the ward accompanied by family who wept, lay curled up on the Quiet Room couch, talked in tense knots in the lounge of Intensive Care, or paced the hall, knuckles white around styrofoam cups. After three or four days this gave way to surprisingly philosophical arrivals of extended family and friends bearing knitting, books, newspapers, special drinks, lotions and walkmans. A patient had settled in for a long haul or recovery from surgery when regular visitors showed confidence in the staff kitchen or knew how to get extra cartons of milk between meals.

Dr. Chambers had been more or less lucid, if weak and unenthusiastic, for several days. He had been moved out of Intensive Care into a room. The room was flooded constantly with visitors, calls, cards, flowers, plants, fruit baskets, children's scrawled drawings, chocolates and magazines: in his case, due to the rate at which news travelled between city and country, attentions never tapered off. Focal point of a diverse flow of humanity, his over-attended recuperation seemed to leave the staff amazed; an exception was two younger nurses Dr. Chambers himself had delivered as babies in the country. Friendly and talkative young women, they remembered him with fondness, in conjunction with head colds and spills from toboggans.

Watching the flowers and visitors arrive, Bea knew them for the measure of her father's garrulous life. She would look at the cards strung above his head or spilling over surfaces, the parading faces ringed round his bed, and feel a net drawn tight; she would fill with resentment for his absence, his inability to measure himself, to know what those watching over him now felt. Her father was weak and vague. With the strange exception of her mother, whom he took for granted, he would greet everyone with his usual host's welcome and a ghost of his old ebullience; then, tiredness would creep over him, visible as a tide, and his speech would lose focus, become forced and elliptical. Dropping the thread of conversations he would mention horses, ask about the stable, who was riding, if the tack had been cleaned. Though he remembered things far back he had little memory for the day-to-day. They would ask him each morning what he had had for breakfast while the plate of pancakes, a bowl of cereal, were freshly pushed aside on his bed tray. "Oh," he'd say. There would come a moment of blankness carefully covered over. "Grapefruit, eggs, sausage, toast... bacon. Coffee."

"Was it good?"

"Uh-hunh." He said it without interest. He was not eating much. Often he would try to give his food away. Formerly he had been known for finishing other people's: *Wall– all right. No point letting it go da waste.*

Family members who lived out of town went back to their jobs. They phoned daily or returned on weekends. Jeffrey and Diane slotted the hospital into work days by speeding over on the subway at lunchtime and bringing bags of take-out after six to eat by Henry Chambers' bed. Their visiting was often a matter of overseeing their father's popularity. The family had become somewhat notorious on the ward. A toothless old man in the bed next to Bea's father grew so stimulated by the incidental company that he uncurled from his foetal position, stopped requesting diapers, and began wearing his teeth and complaining about the food. He called her father "Henry," treating him like an old pal; he would come to visit him in his wheelchair across the ten feet that separated their beds dressed up in his best slippers and dressing-gown with his hair freshly slicked down. The Chambers children had felt sorry for the old man's lack of visitors (a stroke victim, he'd been there too long) and had drawn him some pictures of his own which they'd taped to the wall by his clothes locker. Someone else had given him Henry's extra balloons and pots of tulips.

They had arranged it so that someone always stayed until

visiting-hours ended or Dr. Chambers slept, whichever came last. It was actually inconceivable to them that their father should at any time be left alone. Uncle Luther came from Montreal and lectured them that Henry's type of injury required quiet and rest; his musical voice, subdued but stern, nevertheless betrayed understanding that this advice would be ignored. He was correct. It was not wilful disobedience: to the Chambers, the idea of their father without company for a day seemed the epitome of neglect. Uncle Luther said nothing more. He remained concerned but not anxious. His brother's injuries were carefully explained to him and also to their cousin, a plastic surgeon who specialized in trauma, and Luther and the cousin spent an afternoon in the lounge talking at great length and in technical detail about the possible future operations Henry might require to repair his head and eye socket. The cousin, also, suggested to Bea and her brothers that Henry had too many visitors; he suggested it with even less expectation of results.

Uncle Luther went to say goodbye.

"Well Henry," he chirruped, "I think I'll be on my way now. You've got an awful pile of visitors here," and he winked, clasping Bea's shoulders.

Her father lifted himself shakily onto his elbows. His face, misshapen and purple, rearranged into his best smile. "Awful good a you da come, Luther," said her father. "Nice a you da drop by."

"You get well now," said her uncle, reaching for his coat, and her father said "Say. Luther-."

"Yes?"

"What was the name a that horse?"

There was a silence. Her mother sat wan and embarrassed at the head of the bed. Arthur left the doorway abruptly. Bea remembered the red lunge line, the idea of it: her revolutions and how it felt, ending at Luther's voice.

"Which horse was that, Henry?" asked her uncle.

"Yer horse. Yer big one."

"Mackie?"

"His... You know– his other name."

"Show-name! Windermere's Golden Mackerel!" Uncle Luther said clearly. He said it loudly, musically, with emphasis: as
if responding to flattery.

Occasionally it was possible to get quiet in the room, but this
never lasted long. Liam would arrive, Rainer would phone from
Sydney, Duncan or Donald from California, Francis and his
family from Saskatchewan, and talk would start up again. Dr.
Chambers would take the phone. "How are you!?" he'd ask
absurdly, voice quavering slightly. "Oh, I'm okay. Gittin' better
every day. Good da hear yer voice!" After a minute he would
grow tired. "Wall, nicea you da call," he'd say and hand over the
phone. He would reach for someone's hand. Arthur held his
sausage fingers. Later in the hall Arthur embraced their mother
and sniffed quietly into his beard. Arthur, shyest of them all, had
not done these things in fifteen years: it was a universal Chambers preference to release feelings privately, later, rather than in
public or at the actual onset of distress. This gained them a
reputation for calm efficiency in crisis, but exacted a toll on their
nerves: besides Bea, several of her brothers– Arthur, Rainer,
Duncan– suffered from a certain hyper-awareness of nuance.
Their father shifted restlessly and pulled out his IV needle, and
when nurses got fed up, putting mitts on him so he couldn't
grasp things, Bea received these indignities personally with a
vicarious embarrassment crippling in its intensity. Her father
only turned to her with his one good eye, face now a mask of
brown and green, and said in a low tone meant to be reassuring:
"How are you today, dear? Are you still seeing that doctor?" his
voice flattening with effort. He would close his eyes. "Wall– think
I'll have a rest now," he'd announce abruptly. Five minutes later
he would sit up, reach for a kleenex, spit, and recline again. His
eyes would drift towards the window. "Let's see... There was
Duchess, Bounder... Nika... No... Bones... Coco..." The list
obsessed him. Feeling something missing he would start over.

After a long day Bea's father would cheat on his list and add
in at random the names of friends' horses and the names of

breeds. "Burl Adams' horse, Rosie... Father's first mare, the scrawny one, Nellie. Mother liked her... Tally... Percheron... Thoroughbred... Hunter Cross... Tass... Coco... Standardbred... Saddlebred... Hanoverian... Bones." He would ask for his hearing aid. Now that the swelling had gone down a little he was able to wear it; he would screw it in with a careful, intent expression on his face and adjust the volume, performing these acts, semi-prone in bed, with a confidence in the face of the arcane that momentarily roused Bea's spirits. "How's that new saddle of yer friend's working out?" he would ask. "The Stuben? Worth the money?"

If he already had his hearing aid in, he would take it out. He would hand it to Bea silently, trusting her to put it in its box. Her mother had replaced his shattered glasses with a pair of old ones and he would hand her these too; perversely, his battered eye, which doctors had expected him to lose, remained better than the uninjured one. Then he would roll over. Bea could not get over the vulnerability expressed in her father's figure when he turned to lie on his side. The hospital gown gaped in back; his freckled skin showed in the gap down to the band of the sheet. Under a pastel hospital coverlet, one leg, knee bent, fell over the other in outline. A sausage hand curled at his cheek. He would close his eyes, face now naked without his glasses. She would consider her father's nakedness. She would grow adamant with love, lest someone else watching condescend to pity him. He would begin to drone the names of their horses. "That right?" he would ask when he reached the end.

Bea's mother looked at Bea, waiting. At the foot of the bed Jeff grimaced, shrugging into his overcoat, eyes on the floor; in a vinyl chair by the head of the bed Liam began to fiddle with a spoon.

"Except Bones," Bea said. "Bones comes before Nika. An' you left out Roo."

When Bea grew too big for ponies her father took her horse hunting. By then he wanted a horse too: what he had always yearned for finally came within the grasp of his imagination, and so on balmy spring days when the warmth shimmered the pavement outside her classroom window and breeze scattered chokecherry blossom in the ditch, she'd see her father's car pull into the school on its way home from hospital rounds for lunch. There would come a knock at her classroom door. Her teacher would go to answer it; the class would wait as one person, breathless. Then the teacher would call Bea. Bea would go back to the door, all eyes on her. She would find her father. Standing in the school hall he seemed to dwarf things; although he wasn't particularly tall, the fountain outside the door hovered somewhere around his knees. "Wouldja like da come horse hunting this afternoon?" he'd ask Bea eagerly.

Bea would feel herself lift and tilt. She'd take in her friends' envious faces, the smell of paper and chalk already grown distant with freedom, and they'd be on the road rolling through countryside. They followed directions from some phone call, paraphrased in his illegible scrawl. Bea would decipher the directions out loud while they looked for signs: paddocks full of jumps, low-slung arenas; pictures, on barns, of horses at extended trot, or the grazing bodies and upflung heads of ponies in fields.

This was how they found Bones. Bea, age 12, climbed onto his dappled gold back in the dust of a scorching summer day. They trotted the dimensions of an outdoor ring past the chipped red and white paint of practice hurdles while a plume of dust rose lazily behind his solid hooves. The next day they brought him home. While in the trailer, Bones removed his halter; the first morning Bea went out to feed him she found him wandering the downstairs of the stable, pleased with himself. She shortly discovered that any time she put him outside he would push open the latch with his nose or, as a last resort, jump the fence. In fact Bones would jump anything, often in pursuit of food; he had won jumper classes in jump-offs where hurdles went over five feet and the other entries were thoroughbreds standing sixteen hands high.

He also knew everything a pony could know about people. In

spite or perhaps because of being too smart in this respect, Bones looked after Bea like a nanny until her knowledge of horses began to match his own knowledge of people. At that point he became ornery and bored and had to be sold; until then, on Bones, Bea went from a rider who was all elbows and flying hair to a composed if slouching figure who could manoeuvre around jump-courses, canter without effort across ditches and creeks, or thunder, hunched up like a jockey, down the icy road from Charlene's barn to hers in under ten minutes flat. She could ride or jump bareback, and post without stirrups or saddle; she could make Bones move from gait to gait with signals invisible to the casual eye. Her father bought a horse trailer and she and Charlene skipped school Friday afternoons in autumn to groom their ponies for the fall fairs. They gave them baths and braided their manes and tails, talking around lengths of braiding-thread held in their teeth.

Uncle Luther came to watch her jump.

"Say, that pony loves to jump, doesn't he though?!" Uncle Luther sang out. "And you know, Henry– " Luther dropped his voice for emphasis and Bea's father moved closer to hear: his hearing had just begun to go "– that one's not a bad little rider. Not a bad– lit-tle– rider– atall." He nodded approvingly. Her father looked gleeful. Bea lay back on Bones's rump, let the reins loose, and watched the sky sway above her as Bones walked back to the trailer. In her tack room at home on a piece of binder-twine there was a line of coloured satin rosettes: pink Sixth, green and yellow Fourths or Fifths, a few white Thirds, blue Seconds; and one or two red Firsts, won solely and heroically by Bones himself, in jump-offs during which Bea nearly sailed over his head.

They had still not found a horse for her father. Bea was the test rider before Dr. Chambers felt confident to climb on himself, and so far she had not thought any horse good enough. After they had unloaded and settled Bones from a day at a fair, she would find her father sometimes, sitting in the tack room, a glass of homemade wine in his hand, counting her rosettes.

"Thirteen," he would cry to her. "Yer really doing well." The wine sloshed in his glass. "Seems da me Luther won a ribbon. Fer a pony-race in Gory." He would think for a minute. "Er mebbe that was me."

"*Dad!*" Bea would exclaim, aggrieved. "Don'tjoo *remember?*" He'd grin. "One er the other of us, anyhow," he'd say.

It had fallen to Bea and her mother to fill the long days in her father's hospital room. Technically, Bea did not have to do this. In terms of the family, however, it was taken as obvious that a painter's work was easily set aside in emergencies and further-more, that Bea was her mother's support. As time went on, Dr. Chambers' curious indifference to her mother's attentions in-creased, and Bea came to agree. She and her mother developed routines. They grew proficient at checking menu cards, moving IV poles, unloading meal trays, answering his phone, raising the bed, and interpreting his requests; they found and patronized the nearest and cheapest parking lot, run by a turbaned East Indian grandfather with impeccable old world manners. Each night they drove back to Bea's apartment, where Claudine Chambers would call friends and relatives with progress reports. If she was talking to a very close friend she might break down on the phone; otherwise, like him, Bea's mother did not cry for herself. She took her husband's indifference as a passing symp-tom of injury, and though lack of praise tended to oppress her, bore it with little or no comment: her famous determination simply expanding to fill the gap left by the departure of her greatest admirer.

While climbing into nightgowns and brushing their teeth, they would discuss Dr. Chamber's state. They were careful always to be more hopeful than things really warranted. Bea recognized their behaviour from the mother of the tattooed boy, the parents of the fat woman in a coma: it was the descent of awful hope, the only thing left if you were not to succumb to loneliness. Succumbing to Truth was not so bad– your son will not smile again, your daughter will not wake up or care about her life– ; but the loneliness Truth brought was something else. Loneliness had the power to erase whomever had been left behind.

There came a day when Bea began noticing a steady leeching-out of her father's remaining liveliness. His anxious hospitality grew intermittent and then disappeared. Following it went his sense of humour. His face seemed to lose contour as if eroding; she found herself recalling the girl in the coma. Bea said nothing, not wanting to add to her mother's burdens. His first morning on the ward the nurses had come in at six a.m. to find him missing: a panicked search uncovered that he had removed his intravenous needle, which had been poorly inserted and was hurting him, and climbed over the end of his bed (the bedrails were up) to take a shower. For ten days he had been celebrated as the fittest man of his age they'd ever seen, comparing favourably with 40-year-olds; now, at the family's regular evening assessments, extravagant pronouncements faded. Three days after Bea first noticed the change, everyone else admitted that Dr. Chambers was definitely worse. Doctors noticed also: he was sent for more scans. In the half day during which they awaited results, Dr. Chambers lost all character. He expressed no emotion whatever and ate mechanically, unable to identify what he was eating; it became difficult to tell if he really heard. He called them by the wrong names. He turned to Jeff. "Is your mother done that course she was taking, Andrew?" he murmured politely, without interest.

The neurosurgeon arrived and consulted Claudine. He was a slight, gentle man with greying beard who talked about short-term memory loss, lack of affect, and alterations to the speech area of the brain. The pressure of the clot was increasing. They had decided to operate. They would open a window in the skull, he said, they would suck out the clot, which unless exposed to air was not hard but soft like jelly. It was a straightforward procedure. Most likely the family would see a dramatic improvement in a couple of days. The other possibility was that in a patient of Dr. Chambers' age they would see complications: pneumonia after anaesthetic, heart failure. Bea learned that her father had had a heart condition for some time which he'd never mentioned. The operation was scheduled for next morning. Claudine Chambers went down to the hospital at six am. Bea stayed away. She was painting.

She and her mother had dozed fitfully the night before in Bea's rickety iron bedstead. The bedstead had been rescued by Bea from an abandoned shed against the will of Jeff and Duncan, who had helped carry it away; only her father had thought it was a good idea. Her brothers pointed out that Henry was not a fair judge, since he himself was notorious for keeping things: finding uses for them years after the clutter had exasperated everyone else. "What're you doing?" he would call out, affronted. "Lookit-that's perfectly good!" His own father and several of Bea's brothers, though unfortunately not Jeffrey or Duncan, shared this tendency to collect things. Bea had wire-brushed the rust off the bed, primed and painted it, brought it to the city in a lover's van. The lover had been a mistake and the bed was for the place she had taken after finally leaving him and she had a soft spot for it, believing it to be her first important independent creation. She and her mother had talked a little before sleep. "I hope everything goes well, Mum." "Me too, sweetheart." "Will it take long?" "Mostly to open the skull and sew him up again. The operation doesn't take long." "He'll do all right." Though reticent at other times they were direct and comforting when frightened. They held each other's hands. They embraced for a time. Bea's mother sniffled quietly once or twice. Then her mother turned to sleep. In her shoulders, rounded from inherited bad posture, Bea recognized Henry's helplessness.

Exactly a year after buying Bones, Bea and her father had found Lily. Lily was a champion hunter mare who had been in semi-retirement as a result of bowed tendons; she was tall but short-bodied, compact, with a rocking gait and a wide barrel. The owners had been using her as a brood mare and were now retiring to Florida. In a small muddy barnyard in late March, Bea had climbed onto Lily's broad back, an inch lower than she would sit on her uncle's horse in his neat paddock, felt the great white mare's hobby-horse canter, and known.

As time went on they realized that Lily had the most beautiful face they were likely ever to see on a horse. Wide forehead, mobile ears, gentle, soft, enormous eyes, her expression was always alert, kind, and something else. Bea remembered it now as sadness: an awareness too great for the body of a horse, like someone, turned into an animal, who knew how to talk but couldn't.

Her father was not the best rider. Though nothing would unseat him, he tended to be faintly clumsy with his hands and had trouble keeping his heels down; his centre of gravity often located itself a bit too far back. In his usual vague way he remained oblivious to this. From Lily's back he checked fences and trees, surveyed the pastures and pond, coming in from a ride with a list of jobs he called five minutes long which took half a day each. Lily forgave Dr. Chambers his eccentricities of riding-style. She stood still under his haphazard brushing (Bea would sometimes groom her afterwards), extended her patience for his sketchy work with the tail-comb, tolerated his habit of making the girth one hole too tight. She carried him sturdily, down concessions, across fields, around paddock and woods, lifting and placing large black hooves in a plunging trot. She splashed calmly through puddles and hopped fallen tree trunks. She liked other horses and was generally liked by them; if Bea and her father rode together she was polite to Bea's pony and later to Nika, Bea's flighty chestnut thoroughbred. When the grandchildren began to walk, Lily carried them three in a row on her broad back as carefully as if they were eggs. Dr. Chambers conceived a shy but overriding love for Lily. He would clump down the wooden ramp into the stable with a windfall apple. "Hi-there Lily," he would cry musically. He would reach a bulky arm through the bars, feed her the apple, and scrub her forehead. Lily would lean her head down, prick her agile ears forward, gaze at him wide-eyed while she crunched, whiskers quivering. He had given her the foaling stall, because it was the largest one in the barn. The other stalls were now filled with boarders. He would pull one white ear and murmur half-absently: "How are you, girl? Eh?"

He did not ride often. He liked to go with Bea and by then she was in high school, her riding reduced to short jaunts on weekends, if then. Her riding had fallen off. Sometimes even now Bea was at a loss over just what had happened. She had reached age fifteen and discovered nervousness: horses suddenly made her anxious, heights and distances turned transparent. Bea thought of this fear as failure, and the stable became a threatening place. The sense of failure began to dog her; her interest in drawing increased, an outlet for confusion. She had entered some dim place. She did not know why. There was a man, a friend of the family, who kept his horse at the Chambers' farm and began to grasp Bea in corners. The world impinged.

Reality found out and penetrated the innocent, wholly eccentric world of Bea's family. Charlene put on eye-shadow and bleached her hair. Her pals smoked, bought tight jeans, smiled eagerly at boys. Only Bea did not translate. Pretending to laugh she fought off the man who liked to grab her. She slung bales down the hatch from the mow to the stable, shovelled sawdust off the delivery truck, mucked stalls, came in from the barn and scrubbed her face, surrounded by brothers to whom she now felt inferior. She had seen the girls in tight jeans. She had felt the man's need. It had nothing to do with horses. Horses could not help her.

Bea was not unaware that only a year after her father had gotten his horse, her own interest was toppling. Sometimes she would feel guilty about this. Then she would feel sorry. Then she would push away all feelings, go out once or twice a week to pick Nika's hooves. It was all right. She was fifteen. She was falling from somewhere, not even knowing why; she could command her father not to cry for himself. Every day he would clean Lily's feet before turning her out, and let her back in at dark rattling a juice tin of oats. The white mare would amble in from the barnyard, pause at his solid figure to nudge his pockets for apples, clop to the open door of her stall.

Her father had got Roo from a field of mongrel horses up the road. In the overgrown orchard of a farm gone to seed, skinny horses turned out together bred and inbred year after year. He'd felt pity for them, left out in all weathers and starved; he'd offered the people who owned them, who were poor and lived no better than their horses, the use of his back pasture for the summer. "Wall I knew Bob didn't have any money," he cried, explaining it to them later over lunch, "so I said d'im 'Gimme a horse an' we'll call it quits.'" A girl with black hair, who went to Bea's school and never spoke, trotted Roo down the five miles bareback with a rope round the horse's nose. She climbed oft, slapped Roo's neck silently, and walked away. Roo was a tall gold and white yearling with a springing step, and they discovered that no-one could get near her.

Bea fed in those years. It was before they had automatic watering bowls and every morning she lugged a huge black rubber pail, brimming with icy water, from the barn tap to each stall. The unwatered horses waited nickering, heads hanging over their doors. At first Roo was shy to drink. Bea would stand very still holding the pail, stirring the water with one hand and singing. Alone in the barn, in the morning half-light, she felt safe; it did not occur to her yet there might be some place else to be. Roo would step forward one hoof at a time. She would luff at the water and throw her head up, waiting to be startled. Bea didn't move. She stood stock-still, singing. Roo would lower her head, luff once more, then thrust her soft muzzle onto the top of the water. She would drink in long heedless gulps while Bea balanced the lightening pail against the door and stroked the white blaze down Roo's face. Roo would lift her head finally, whiskers dripping, and let a little water from her mouth dribble back into the pail. She would lip Bea's sleeve cautiously. She would tug on it with her teeth. Bea would blow towards her nostrils and Roo would arch her neck carefully and blow back.

After a week or two Bea would open the door and water Roo standing just inside the stall. If she finished feeding early she would go in, crouch down by the stone wall, and sing to herself. The straw crackled where she crouched in her torn barn jacket; Roo stood close with a mouthful of hay, breathing into Bea's hair.

Bea never got on her back.

Her brothers did; and when Roo bucked them off, her father sold Roo to a woman with an arena. Roo, he told the new owner, preferred women. Sometimes in the mornings Bea would crouch in Lily's stall singing. Lily didn't mind.

The next year Dr. Chambers spent in Toronto. Four of Bea's brothers were in university and did not qualify for student loans; their father had decided to pick up anaesthesia in order to earn more money. Claudine Chambers stayed home at the farm, chairing a fund drive.

There was a boy who mucked stalls on alternate days. One evening in March he came to the door. Lily was cast in her box, he said. She was trembling and sweaty; she hadn't eaten anything since yesterday and she wouldn't drink. Claudine called the vet. The vet arrived. He ran his hands and stethoscope over the lathered form prone in the straw and drew of a lethal dose of anaesthetic. Lily had an aneurism. It was too late. He might have saved her, he said, if she'd shown distress earlier. The trouble was, her pain threshold was too high.

Dr. Chambers came home from the city grey and quiet. Bea's mother confided to Bea that he hadn't slept since she'd phoned him with the news. He stood staring blankly at the vet's bill on the desk, where her mother had put it intending to hide it. He'd wished she hadn't phoned at all, Claudine told Bea. Why? Bea had wondered. Bea was at school when it happened; she had not seen Lily's body. She had wept that night crouched by the wall in Lily's straw. Her father went abruptly to the pantry and poured himself a drink. He went down to the basement. After a time they heard him clanking bottles in the workbench. Because, said her mother, he felt helpless. He kept thinking she was only fifteen and how much he hates that city.

Next morning, when Bea went out to feed, her father was already there. He sat very still, on the bench outside Lily's stall. He liked to sit there in the evenings, to gossip with boarders. Lily would poke her muzzle through the bars and lip at his toque. He said to Bea loudly: "We've had some good animals, haven't we?" Bea nodded. He still sat. "Luther really liked that horse," he said. "Luther- thought- the world- a Lily." "Have you fed grain, Dad?" Bea asked. He nodded, looking lost. When she went to stand near him, she saw in Lily's feedbox a fresh pile of oats. She waited another year to tell him she had finished with horses.

With her mother snoring beside her in Toronto Bea fell asleep. She dreamed it was spring and she and her father were in the woods at the farm. They had gone back to cut a new bridle path: the old one, cut by Rainer and Duncan, had somehow grown in. She and her father tacked back and forth through the woods, looking for its traces, calling out to each other. "It used to go here!" "It went this way!" "I remember this!" In his preoccupied way her father bent back branches to mark the route; he told her they should cut now, before leaves came on the trees and the markings got lost. The day began to wane. They reached a wall of grapevines and raspberry canes. Neither of them could tell which direction the old trail had gone. Each time they tried to continue they were stopped by underbrush and would find themselves back in the same small clearing. Around them the great beech trees lifted their grey trunks into spring evening air. A few left over leaves, bleached by winter to the colour of parchment, clung to an etching of twigs low down on one trunk. The leaves trembled in a cool breeze. The air was damp with the smell of melted earth. They stood on a bit of higher ground, looking at each other in a rustling underpad of dead leaves. Bea began to speak.

Her father's expression did not change. Bea spoke louder. He looked at her without moving and then she realized, beginning to sob, that he could no longer hear. He was stone deaf. She fell onto her knees and dropped her head to the ground.

When she looked up again her father had brightened. He broke into a grin and set off once more, up a path that opened suddenly behind him. The sun reached the horizon. Tilting through the trees it sent oblique shadows across the forest floor and fell past her father's knees and her feet and the roots and brambles in long low beams of evening fire. She watched her father go away, bending branches carelessly down on either hand for her to follow. His favourite old corduroys drooped in the bum and everywhere he walked leaves sticking up were tipped with gold by slanting light, so that it seemed as if he meandered, single-minded as always, between a thousand candles.

Bea stayed at home painting. There was a maze of legs. Grey, white, chestnut, gold, sinews taut from fetlock to haunch. Through the middle of them all, disappearing and reappearing, ran a red line in broken peaks and valleys.

Uncle Luther had bought Nika. Later he sold her to an equestrian student who moved away to Calgary and two years after that Dr. Chambers came across a new horse for himself without Bea's help, and without really looking, and bought her on the spot for too much money. The mare was young and green then, but she looked like Lily. It was ten years since Bea had had a horse of her own. Lately, on weekends at the farm, she would saddle up whatever horse she could borrow.

Bea had come round to things. She had come round to seeing that she could now ride with any proficiency at all because for no reason she knew of except compassion her father had got her in on Charlene's lessons. Twice a week they had loaded Duchess up in a rickety old trailer he borrowed from a junk man up the road and then they had driven ten miles to a farm outside the next town; there they would back in beside Charlene's gleaming trailer and unload for a two hour lesson so that by the time her friends were dreaming of horses in the fierce outlines of adolescent fantasy, Bea was riding Duchess up and down the miles of concession roads with Charlene and Coco as carelessly as a travelling salesman.

They had kept sets of clothes exclusively for the stable. The smell of horse, thick and acrid-sweet, had never left the folds except immediately after washing; Charlene's mother had made her keep hers in the back porch but Bea's had hung on the peg in her closet. Manure was caked permanently in the treads of their stable boots. They had grown small bulging muscles from hefting manure forks, wheel-barrows, slinging bales of hay. Pine tar hoof-polish made black crescent moons under their finger-nails. From the backs of ponies they discussed boys, kids at school, rock stars they had crushes on; the poor family that lived next door to Charlene, and, cautiously, their parents. They stole apples from peoples' orchards standing up in their stirrups. They went into Thomasons' field and pretended to round up cows and the cows stared at them before slowly heaving into a lumbering gallop for one or two strides. They were buzzed by young toughs driving souped-up cars. Faces stiffly forward they raced parallel to the toughs along the ditches before swerving down some laneway with a departing lift of their middle fingers. They bent round Hurlbuts' crooked mailbox. They took the muddy lane to the Chambers' woods and rode through shade swatting at overhanging green branches planning adult lives full of glamour, large horses, and smouldering but clean and obedi-ent men. Their futures turned on what they knew. Ponies walking loose, reins not held at all, their legs swinging free of the stirrups: the ponies were also them. It was the moment before the aneurism, the freedom before life or sex dictated their descent to the ground. The ponies lowered their heads to slurp at the stream, their manes fell forward and they gulped, rattling their bits; Charlene or Bea would dig her heels in as chestnut or grey head came round and they would bound through the stream, rocks rattling under pony-shoes. If it rained they pulled off saddles and bridles and leather boots, and rode bareback with streaming toes.

Between the ages of nine and fourteen their tiredness had been

clean and without exhaustion. They were not bored. They had
sat after a full day's riding in one or the other's barn, soaping
saddles and bridles, pretending they were professional grooms,
and when a bell rang for supper they had walked up in the dusk
to whatever house it was, the insides of their thighs, their knees
and calves, streaked with grey or chestnut hairs. Her father had
given her all this. She had not even really had to ask. Once her
father had wanted it for himself but his father, the beatings in
the woodshed, Luther's or his own, what he had forgiven, had
stopped him.

The phone rang. Bea's machine kicked in. She found herself
whispering. Mack, Corgi, Bounder, Duchess, Bones, Roo, Nika,
Lily. *Luther. Luther. Luther.*

Her Uncle Luther came on the machine. In the background
she could hear her mother. "We're calling to tell you Beatrix,"
said her uncle's formally modulated voice, "that your father
pulled through his surgery just fine. He's out of the recovery
room now and they've got him in Intensive Care."

Her father left Intensive Care for the second time within a
matter of hours. He now sported his own silo-roof bandage, but
it was bending one of his ears down so he got Liam to help him
take it off. No-one reprimanded him. Nurses adjusted drip
medication and departed. He began once again surpassing all
records for his age.

Underneath the silo bandage his head had been half-shaved.
A long incision ran across the site of his injury, which was closed
with a row of metal staples, and Bea and her brothers joked to
him about Frankenstein, looking for bolts in his neck as they
rubbed lotion into his elbows against the recent onset of bed-
sores. They told him the shaved part made him look like Yoda
from *Star Wars*. Bea remembered her parents going to see *Star
Wars*. Her mother had said it was fun; her father had grimaced,
biting his tongue judiciously, and waved one mitt-like hand in
dismissal. "Far's I could figger out it was jist a lotta shooting an'
killing," he'd said.

173

With renewed vigour the Chambers and their relatives mobbed Henry's hospital room. Uncle Luther had stayed on. They watched eagle-eyed for signs of the promised dramatic change; though Claudine was convinced it set in immediately, to Bea and her brothers the change came after several days. Jeffrey had walked into the room. He and Diane had requested a moment alone. They had told him they were expecting a baby and that Henry would have to teach it to ride and he had broken into a smile, they said; when the others came back he was weak and gleeful, exclaiming in his singsong voice "Well isn't that the greatest news!" as if for years there hadn't been any. Only his hearing was not better; someone gave him his hearing aid, he screwed it in with phantom eagerness, and they began to shout.

The old man from the next bed wheeled over to salute Dr. Chambers with one skinny hand. Then he drew Bea aside. He adjusted his teeth, which were slightly too big, and looked up at her seriously. "Henry tole me the list last night," he whispered to her loudly. "I thoughtja might like ta know." Bea bent a little closer. He drew himself up, licking his lips, and began rhyming off on long thin fingers. "Corgi, Bounder, Duchess, Bones, Roo, Nika, Beatrix, an' Lily. Then there's'is present horse, one'e fell offa. That there's a white mare too but she's got the name a Charlemagne. Charlemagne. Some French king. He says," one finger stabbed towards Henry's bed, "guy that named'er thought it was a drink." He added: "Don't let on, but it bugged'im'e always fergot her." He paused. "Well? Did'e get it right fine'ly?"

Bea stood looking down at him. He was waiting. She gave a nod. The old man shook her hand solemnly, one veteran to another, and wheeled off down the hall for a smoke.

The day they discharged Dr. Chambers it was grey and overcast, the city teeming with cars backed up in a dump of melting snow. Christmas decorations had been put up and they banged in a warm wind against streetlight poles. Bea sat with him by the front entrance in a heap of plants and flower containers. One hardy balloon was tied to the arm of his wheelchair. Nearby stood a white statue in marble of the hospital's patron saint, St. George; he vanquished a rather small dragon from the back of a stallion with a roman nose. A car horn tooted. Bea helped her father out of his chair and down the worn steps into the street. Dr. Chambers paused, looking up at the nearby office block. Blood under his face, renewed by the surgery, lay in two black smudges below his eyes; where the breaks had healed, his temple was caved in and one eyelid drooped. "Say, I'll be glad da git home," he cried. "I couldn't stand lookin' at that damn building." He reached, fumbling, for the car door which her mother had pushed open.

Bea gave him a leg-up and rode with him. They trotted the lane past the pond, through the woods, around the field and back, beside thistles and cornstalks left by the harvester. At the rear pasture her father reined in. "Oh say lookit," he said. "That pasture hasda be burned off before the new grass comes in." She began to picture this and he added automatically, "A course, yer mother'll say it's a waste a time."

"Oh Dad," Bea said distinctly. "That's just not true." He didn't hear her. He turned his horse, already forgetting; they trotted up towards the barn, Dr. Chambers bouncing a little as he posted, and Bea saw how it would turn out. It would be spring. Liam or Jeffrey or Bea herself would help. They would stand ready against accidents with the old rust-coloured canvas hose, attached to a pump and feeding from the pond. Her father would walk out through the tongues of fire. He would walk out of hearing range, the length of the horse pasture and back: shifting in the smoke, concentrated, droning, lighting the weeds where they hadn't caught.